SIX MONTHS TO LIVE

CHARLES SNYDER

The nutritional and health information in this book is based on the teachings of God's Holy Word, the Bible, as well as research and personal experience by the author and others. The purpose of this book is to provide information and education about health. The author and publisher do not directly or indirectly dispense medical advice or prescribe the use diet as a form of treatment for sickness without medical approval. Nutritionists and other experts in the field of health and nutrition hold widely varying views. The author and publisher do not intend to diagnose or prescribe. The author and publisher intend to offer health information to help you cooperate with your doctor or other health practitioners in your mutual quest for health. In the event you use this information without your doctor's or health practitioner's approval, you prescribe for yourself. This remains your constitutional right. The author and publisher assume no responsibility.

Authored by Charles Snyder

Layout and Design by **AdvanceGraphics** (www.advancegraphics.us)

First printing 2005

ISBN 0-929619-21-8

This Edition Published and Distributed by

Hallelujah Acres Publishing
P.O. Box 2388
Shelby, NC 28151
704-481-1700

Visit our web site at www.hacres.com

Contents

Dedication and Foreword

This book is dedicated to the thousands of Health Ministers℠ around the world, who are working to teach millions of people suffering from disease, how to get well.

The characters are fictional, though they represent testimonies of people who saved their lives by adopting God's plan for radiant health.

All the teachings are based on fact. Our bodies were designed to live without disease. We suffer because we depart from that design.

The characters in this book go to a fictional island. However, Hallelujah Acres Lifestyle Centers℠ are being developed all over the world where the truth that, You Don't Have to be Sick℠, is being taught. It is also taught that, once you do get sick, there is a better way to deal with disease. By returning to the diet and lifestyle our bodies were designed for.

The main characters in this book are thrust into this lifestyle through no choice of their own. You however have a choice. In this book, you will learn about a real organization that is making a difference in peoples' lives.

Part of the profit from this book will help a Health Minister℠ near you.

I hope you enjoy this book as much as I enjoyed writing it.

—*Charles Snyder*

chapter one

Retirement

Adam and Eve Westbrook represent a typical couple from the baby-boom generation. Adam is sixty-two and Eve is sixty. They have two children, Sue and Larry, and six grandchildren. Adam retired after thirty-five years as an office manager. He made a very good living, so Eve stayed home to raise the kids and take care of their home. They lived in a typical large American town. They were both active in their church. Their life was very normal, until October 2002.

As part of his retirement package, Adam retained his medical coverage. He and Eve had two different doctors who worked in the same office. The first week of October, they went in together for a regular checkup. This is their story, as told by Adam.

Doctor John Murphy, a young man in his early forties, examined me. He asked, "Have you noticed anything you think I should know about, Adam?"

"Well Doc, I have some discomfort in my groin, and shortness of breath if I push myself physically. I can only mow the grass a few minutes at a time."

After the exam, Dr. Murphy told me that he needed to schedule tests, including one for stress.

While I was getting my exam with Dr. Murphy, Eve was with Dr. Mea Storm. She asked, "Have you noticed any new health problems, Eve?"

Eve said, "My arthritis is more painful and I have tenderness in my left breast." She pointed to the spot.

After Eve got dressed, Doctor Storm came back into the examining room. She said, "Eve, your diabetes is worse and I feel a lump in your left breast. I need to schedule you for x-rays and other tests."

I took Eve to get her x-rays and tests on the following Monday. Eve took me for my tests on Tuesday.

On Thursday, Doctor Murphy told me that I had clogged arteries and prostate cancer. I needed an operation for both as soon as possible. The earliest we could schedule the surgery was the first week of November.

He advised me not to perform any more strenuous physical activity before the day of the surgery. "We can fix your heart problem," he said, "but with your prostate cancer being so advanced, I can only give you a twenty percent chance to live another six months to a year."

Eve got her bad news on Thursday evening, with me by her side, holding her hand sitting in Doctor Storm's office. Doctor Storm said, "Eve, you have advanced breast cancer in both breasts. Even if we operate, I can't give you a very good prognosis. We need to schedule a radical mastectomy of both breasts and chemo. The soonest we can schedule your operation is the first week of November. With the complication of your diabetes, I can't give you much hope."

"So, what are my chances, Doctor Storm?" Eve asked.

"Without treatment, I would say you have six months to live. If you survive treatment, we may be able to add a year to that time."

That evening we met with our pastor and told him,

"Pastor Crane, I worked thirty–five years to pay off our home and save enough for us to retire in comfort, and now this. It is just not fair. Why would God allow this? We could both be dead by Thanksgiving. That would be less than four months from the day I retired. I just don't see how this could be for our good. One or both of us will most likely not live out the year. What should we do?"

"Well, Adam, I know both you and Eve have been praying. We will start the prayer chain for you. Your efforts on behalf of the community have made you loved by many in this state. I will contact the pastors in our state association so their congregations will pray for you as well. Also, I have an idea. You know I have been praying about your situation for over a week now. You still own a seaplane, don't you?"

"Yes, Pastor, we do," I replied.

"Your surgeries are not for three weeks. Why don't you and Eve fly down to the Virgin Islands for a two–week vacation, have some fun, and take your mind off your problems?"

"Pastor, that sounds like a great idea. Eve, what do you think?"

Eve said, "I think it is a great idea, too. I just hope Sue and Larry don't get upset about us leaving at a time like this."

When we got home, we called Sue and Larry and asked them to come over. They arrived about 9:00 p.m. We went into the dining room and sat at the table.

I said, "Kids, we received some bad news today. We thought we should tell you right away, before the prayer chain reaches you. Your mother and I had some tests done and have some alarming news. We both have cancer, and your mother's diabetes is worse, which will complicate her treatment. To top it off, I have blocked arteries. Our doctors don't give either of us much hope that we will survive the treatments."

When the crying subsided a little, I continued, "We met with Pastor Crane today, just before we called you. He informed us that many churches would be praying for us. That gives us a little spark of hope."

Sue said, "Dad, Mom, you two don't look like you are very upset."

I admitted, "Well, we were. Before we called you, we prayed and got some peace from God. We made a decision you may not agree with. Pastor Crane suggested that we fly down to the Virgin Islands for two weeks. He thought some fun in the sun would be good for us. We have three weeks before our surgeries and we thought, why not?"

Sue and Larry looked at each other. A knowing look passed between them, and Larry finally spoke, "Mom, Dad, we think that no one deserves a vacation more than you two. When do you leave?"

"Well, son, we appreciate your support. We expected some protest. We would like to pack tomorrow and leave Saturday. We will spend a day or two at several places along the way. With our old amphibious plane, we can stop just about anywhere if we get tired."

"Sue and I, along with our families, will see you off on Saturday, then. What time do you plan to leave? Do you know where you are going to stop?"

"Well, let's plan on leaving at 8:00 a.m. I think we will stop at Pensacola, Florida, spend the night, and then fly to Cancun, Mexico, on Sunday. We know some missionaries there, so it should be a good visit. We can spend a day with them and then fly to Jamaica. I have a friend from work who lives in Jamaica. From there, we can visit some friends in St. Thomas before we head back, stopping to rest along the way."

On Saturday morning, Sue with her husband and two girls, and Larry with his wife and four boys, met us at the dock behind our home. Sue handed Eve a small package. She said, "Mom, I have early stages of arthritis, as you know. I have been studying natural methods of dealing with it. If you have time, you may want to read this information." Eve thanked her and took the small package. I placed it in the cargo area and secured everything for the trip. We held hands and I prayed:

"Father, we don't understand all this. We trust that we are safe in Your hands. Guard our hearts and increase our faith as we seek to take our minds off our own problems. Show us Your plan for us, Lord, and use us in some way before You take us home to be with You. Please, Lord, watch over our family while we are gone. In Jesus name we pray. Amen."

We hugged our children and grandchildren, got in the plane, and took off.

chapter two

The Adventure Begins

We arrived in Pensacola on schedule about eight hours later. We filled the plane's fuel tanks and found a hotel where we ate and spent the night. In the morning, we checked the plane over and left for Cancun.

In Cancun late that afternoon, we met missionary Pastor Emmanuel Garza and his wife Dar. Later that evening, after the service, we told Emmanuel and Dar about our health problems and why we were taking the trip.

As we sat around the table, Pastor Garza said, "Let us pray together." We all held hands as he prayed:

"Father God, I come to You in the name of our blessed Savior Jesus Christ. You created us. Only You can heal our brother and sister of these diseases. Lord, Your servants have blessed many over the years. They have given of their time, talents, and money to help many who were in need. They have supported this ministry here in Cancun for many years.

"We thank You, Father, for the many years we have known Your servants. We thank You for the love they have shown our people. We thank You for showing us Your power in many ways.

"We ask You, Father, to work a miracle for our brother and sister Westbrook. We know, Father, that medical science has very little to offer. You are the Creator. You designed our bodies. Only You can make them whole again.

"Father, we give our dear brother and sister into Your hands. We don't believe You are ready for their work to end. If we are wrong, Father, please give us the grace to accept Your will. If we are right, we give You the glory and praise for the great work You are about to do. Amen!"

We spent all day Monday together. Pastor Garza and Dar took us on a tour of the city and the surrounding villages. They showed us an orphanage run by Christian brothers and sisters from the local church, and told us our gifts had helped build it.

When we returned to the Garza home that evening, we knew that the pictures we had seen did not do justice to the work that was being done for Christ in Cancun. They did not give us a full sense of the great need. More street children needed to be reached. The stark contrast between the affluent commercial region and the great poverty in the outlying areas shocked us.

When we went to bed that night, we thought about the great burdens of the people of Cancun and the children of the orphanage. We forgot about our own problems as we poured out our hearts to God on behalf of the Garza family and the families of the workers at the orphanage.

chapter three

JAMAICA

The next morning we all got up early. We ate breakfast and prayed together. Pastor and Mrs. Garza took us to our plane. We said our goodbyes and left.

The trip to Jamaica was uneventful. We arrived early in the afternoon. Jim and Sally Baker met us and took us to their home. It was a completely different atmosphere from the one at the Garza home, where the love of Christ was in the air. Here, there was the fellowship of friends, but no love. All the things money could buy were evident. The food was good, the company was pleasant, but the love of Christ was not there.

Jim and Sally showed us the sights of Jamaica and we had a good visit. I tried to talk to Jim about Christ but he was not interested. Eve had the same response from Sally.

That night, we told them about our health problems. Jim said, "Well, my friend, you have the right idea. Go out and have as much fun as you can, while you can. You will be missed."

Later that night in the bedroom, Eve and I were so burdened for the salvation of our lost friends that we forgot our problems and poured out our hearts to God for them. We asked Jesus to work in their hearts. To convict them of their lost condition, and make them see that they needed a savior.

chapter four

Lost at Sea

The next morning, Jim and Sally took us to our plane, wished us an enjoyable trip, and said goodbye.

We got in the plane and took off for St. Thomas. The forecast was for clear skies and light winds all day. We were flying at ten thousand feet. About a half hour out of Jamaica, we saw a haze on the horizon. A few minutes later, it was all around us. I was not worried because I was instrument-rated.

Then we lost all power to the cockpit. The engine kept running, but none of the instruments were working. I did get worried then. It kept getting darker, even though it was before noon. I tried the radio and it was dead. Soon, in only minutes, it was so dark that we could not see anything. We could do nothing but pray, and try to keep the plane level by the sound of the engine.

Hours passed.

Suddenly, the engine started to sputter, and died. Almost immediately, the cloud vanished, as if it had never been there.

I saw a small crescent-shaped island ahead. There was nothing else in view except water. I kept the nose down to maintain air speed, and made for the island. The points of the crescent formed a protected harbor on the west side of the island. I was able to make a soft landing and coast up to the sandy beach in that harbor.

I got out of the plane, got the tie–down ropes out of the cargo compartment, and tied one to the nose of the plane. By tying all three ropes together, I was able to reach a tree close to the beach to secure the plane. I then went back to the plane to get Eve.

When we were both safe on shore on the dry sand, exhausted both physically and mentally, we dropped to our knees to pray:

"Father, God, thank You for giving us this safe landing. Lord, we don't understand what is going on here. I know that was not a normal cloud. I have never heard of a plane losing all power to the instruments like that.

"We understand that You must have a purpose in this. Though we don't understand, we trust You. We surrender to Your will and only seek Your guidance. Show us what to do one step at a time, Father.

Father, please give our family peace. We know that if we don't know where we are, they don't know either, and they will soon be very worried. Amen."

chapter five

No Food In the Plane

Back in the states, Sue and Larry were going nuts trying to find out what happened to us. When we did not arrive at our scheduled destination on time, our old friends Dale and Suzy Thompson called Jim Baker in Jamaica to find out if we had left on time. Suzy then notified our daughter Sue.

She and Larry called everyone they could think of to get a search started. No one gave them much hope. They thought, "What happened? Where are they?"

On the island, the tide was coming in and we were trying to decide where to sleep that first night.

"Eve, I think that when the tide reaches its high point, we should pull the plane in as far as we can and tie it off better, before we look around much. We have some snacks we can eat. I will check the emergency locator and the cell phone to see if we can send a signal or call anyone."

I came back in a few minutes to tell Eve that, not only were all the batteries dead, but the snacks were missing.

I also told her, "This is totally weird. It is almost high tide and we have no food or water. Based on the high water mark, high tide should come in about an hour. Let's explore the beach close to where we are now and see what we can find."

As we walked north, we found banana trees with ripe fruit. We picked some and went back to the plane. We attached the rope to the right wing and pulled the plane close enough to be tied with just one rope. In the process, we spun it around sideways. Then we attached a rope to the tail ring and tied it to another tree.

"OK, Eve, that should do it. We should be able to tilt the seats back and sleep in the plane tonight. With the transponder not working, I don't expect to be rescued any time soon."

As we ate the bananas we found, Eve commented that they were the best-tasting bananas she had ever eaten. I said, "It is probably because they were ripened on the tree." We slept in the plane that first night on the island.

chapter six

New Beginnings

At daybreak, we decided to evaluate our assets. It was a beautiful cloudless day, so we pulled out all the cargo to take inventory. We had plenty of clothes for several weeks. We had two Bibles and the information Sue had given us on health. At the bottom of the pile, we found a survival kit with a knife, hand ax, matches, first-aid supplies, twenty-four 16 oz. bottles of water, and some dried fruit and nuts.

I tried to comfort Eve, "We have enough food for several days. We have tools to build a comfortable shelter. Or should we just stay in the plane?"

Eve said, "I think we should change into clothes more suited to hiking and explore the island."

So we walked to the south point of the island along the shore, and came back up the east side. I had the knife and ax on my belt. To our surprise, the beach was perfect for walking.

I was getting winded, and after an hour of slow walking, we stopped.

"You know, Eve, we could die here. We can't contact anyone. The only way we can send any kind of signal is with a fire. There is one good thing, though. The plane is bright yellow and out in the open. If a plane flies over, they will see it."

"Yes, and I have thought about the fact that the doctor gave us only six months to live if we don't get the surgery we are supposed to get next week. What are we going to do if no one comes for us?"

"All we can do is pray and do what we can to survive."

"So, why don't we pray together right now?" I agreed, and we started praying:

"Lord Jesus, we praise You for Your wonderful creation. We thank You for this island of protection in the midst of the vast ocean. Even though we haven't got a clue as to where we are, we are sure that You know.

"Lord, we could not ask for a more beautiful place to visit. Only You know how long this visit will be. Help us draw closer to You and to each other.

"Lord, we pray for our children and friends. They have to be worried about us. Please, Lord, give them peace. Help them to understand that we are in the center of Your will.

"This is a hard thing for us to comprehend but we know that You don't make mistakes. We believe that You have a greater purpose in our being here. Help us to see that purpose. Help us to trust You each step of each day. Amen.

"Well, dear, let us continue our walk before it gets too hot. We must be about halfway around the island. We have seen a lot of coconut palm trees and a few banana trees. So far, we have seen no wildlife. It is just God, this island, and the two of us."

After another hour, we were back at the plane.

"Adam, how far would you say it is around the island following the beach?"

"Well, we were walking very slow, looking up into the trees and poking around in everything we could see from the beach. I would guess that we were walking at about two miles per hour. That would make it about four miles from the plane all the way around and back again."

Eve said, "Neither of us is used to being out in the sun. It is 10 a.m. and the sun is starting to get very bright. I think we should sit in the plane or under the trees to rest. It will be a great time to read. Let's read the information Sue gave us."

"OK, I will open all the doors and vents and we will see if the plane has enough shade. At least the seats should be comfortable."

"So, what do we have in this package?" Eve wondered. She read the titles of the books: Why Christians Get Sick by Rev. George Malkmus, and Health by Design by Charles Snyder. "Looks like a quick read for both."

Adam and Eve read both books and then re-read them. They got out their Bibles and looked up the Bible references. Adam looked at Eve and asked, "Do you think that God is trying to tell us something we would not have listened to under any other circumstances? We were basically given a death sentence. If what we are reading is true, we were causing our own death. In essence, committing slow suicide by ignorance.

"Here we are with nothing to eat but fruits and perhaps some vegetables. If the rest of this island is anything like what we have seen so far, we are living in an all-you-can-eat smorgasbord with nothing else to do but get a little exercise while we explore the island."

"Yes, Adam, I agree. We were comfortable in our service to our Lord, our community, and our general lifestyle. But these books say, that lifestyle, was causing our health problems. If what we have just read is true, we were indeed eating our way to the grave."

"Well, these pages are giving me hope. I know God is good and He must have a purpose for this. I am now confident that we will receive all the nutrition we need from the food we can find here. So, let's just praise God and start exploring this beautiful island. Perhaps one day soon we will be better servants for this experience."

chapter seven

MOUNTAIN

It took us just two hours to walk around the island. I suggested, "Let's see if we can go straight across the middle."

One hour later, I commented, "this undergrowth is so dense. This is going to take a little longer. We are going uphill. Wow!"

"What is it, Adam? Oh my!" Eve gasped.

"I think this is a volcanic island, and that is the remains of the volcano."

"How are you feeling, Adam? Is your heart bothering you?"

"No. Let's climb a little more, it is still early."

A half-hour later, being careful not to overdo it, we were above the trees, on a slightly curved dome that looked like the volcano made a bubble that was about to pop and cooled suddenly. It was about the size of a helicopter pad on top of a building.

"This is strange," I said, "It is just tall enough to see over the trees but not tall enough to see the beach. We are perhaps fifty feet above the tops of the trees. Sure is a great view. I'm not ready to head back.

Let's sit quietly for a minute to see if we can hear anything besides the ocean and the wind in the trees."

"Adam, I hear running water. It sounds like it is coming from over there."

I was eager to look into it, "Well, let's go down that way. The island is too small to get lost for long."

Though this small volcanic mountain was steep, it was very rough, with places to step and hold on. It was just tall enough for a few hours climbing, but not so tall that you couldn't be back to camp before dark. As we went down, the sound of a small waterfall grew louder. Soon we could see it, just below the tree line. It was a very small stream, about a foot wide and an inch or two deep. It fell into a deep pool about sixty feet in diameter. We came up close, tasted the sweet fresh water, and drank deeply. "Why not go for a swim?" I proposed. Eve happily agreed.

I told her, "OK, let me jump in first to see if we can get out without a problem."

So I jumped in, clothes and all. I remembered swimming in the river at home with my running shoes on, in case there were sharp rocks or broken bottles at the bottom.

The water was cool but not cold. The sides of the pool were steep but easy to climb. It looked like over on the other side it would be easier to get out. I yelled, "Come on in, this is great!"

Eve jumped in, and we enjoyed our swim. About a half-hour later, we swam to the other side. We walked out as if from a swimming pool.

"Well, Eve, it is getting late and we don't know how long it will take to get back to the plane." So we headed back. We could see the top of the mountain through the trees when we started. It was steep, going till we got into the trees, but soon we were back at the plane.

On the way back, we found an unusual fruit we did not recognize. We ate several. It was very sweet and satisfying. By the time we reached the plane, we were more tired than I can ever remember, but we were satisfied and contented, not exhausted.

chapter eight

First Big Challenge

Early the next morning, I woke up with a fever. I ached all over. I was chilled. Eve woke up when she heard me moaning. About then, she ran off to the edge of the trees to a hole I had dug for a latrine. We had no medicine to treat our symptoms so, as the books taught us, we drank water and rested. That was, I think, the hardest thing I had ever asked Eve to do.

All that day, every few minutes, Eve kept going back to the latrine and returning to comfort me. She wrapped me with our one blanket the best she could while we toughed it out. Neither of us felt like eating.

Eve said, "I wish we were back home so I could give you something for your symptoms."

"Not me," I said weakly. "I think this is the healing crisis they talked about in the books we read yesterday. If so, it will soon pass." Late that night, my fever got worse for a while and then broke. I felt weak but somehow better for surviving our first big challenge in our new way of life.

That next morning, I did not feel well enough to do anything, and neither did Eve. She went just inside the tree line and found some oranges, brought them to me, and we ate. Then I decided to do a little planning.

I had a suggestion, "If we are not rescued soon, we will need to set up a more permanent camp on high ground, in case of a tropical storm."

"Yes, Adam, that sounds reasonable."

"It is likely that there are caves in the mountain. We should be close to our fresh water source. If we are both up to it tomorrow, I would like to explore the area around the pool and waterfall. Of course, while we are there, we can go for a swim. How does that sound to you, Eve?"

"Wonderful."

chapter nine

THE CAVERN

We ate breakfast the next day and headed for the pool. We were a little off in our direction but we found it. First, we walked all the way around the lower side. On the waterfall side, the bank was steep and rose sharply from the water.

We searched above the waterfall and all around the pool but found nothing. We were about to give up when Eve noticed movement in the vines hanging over the waterfall. We climbed up to the small stream and looked behind the curtain of vines to discover an opening the size of a doorway.

As we moved into the opening, we noticed that, though it was dark, it was not total darkness, as you would expect in a cave. About thirty feet into the cave, it started to open up. Soon we were in a large pear-shaped cavern, with the entrance being the stem. The stream gurgled up in the center of the large end and flowed out the entrance.

High above, a dull light brightened the entire room. "Eve, I bet that light is the dome we sat on a few days ago. The next time we go up there, let's set a big chunk of bark or something up there. When we come back, we should be able to see it."

I was just guessing, but the room looked about one hundred feet wide and twice that long. While wandering around, we found a fairly level area with a low terrace big enough for a bed. I said, "There could be other openings among the trees on the north end of the mountain. We will have to investigate later. In the evening, we may be able to see light. I think there are small openings because I feel a light breeze.

"We could use this for our home until we are rescued. We could clear a path from the beach to the pool, and place an arrow of some sort for rescuers to find us."

"Sounds good, Adam. How do you feel?"

"That is strange. I really had not thought about it. Well, I am a little tired but not winded. Actually, I feel better than I have in more than a year. How about you, how do you feel?"

Eve smiled, "I feel the same. My breast is not as tender and my arthritis is not as sore. I only have enough diabetes medicine left for a week; it is almost gone. I should start tapering off I suppose. We will just have to pray that, by the time I run out, I will no longer need it."

I answered, "Yes, why not pray right now?" We held hands and prayed:

"Almighty God, as near as we can see, You have created a small paradise, just for us. We don't know what else to say but thank You. And thank You for the improvement in our health. We marvel at the simplicity of Your plan for our health. We have been here ten days. Tomorrow we were supposed to have surgery for our health problems. We believe You have a better plan for us.

"Father, again we pray for our loved ones who don't know that we are safe and alive. Most of them know we love You and would be safe anyway, but only You can comfort them. So, please wrap Your arms around them. In the name of Jesus, our matchless Savior, Amen."

chapter ten

SETTLING IN

On the way back, Eve took the survival knife, I used the hand ax, and we hacked a narrow trail out to the plane. Before leaving the trees, we grabbed some fruit. Then we climbed into the plane for a much needed rest. We ate our meal and read our Bibles until dark.

In the morning, we decided to widen the trail a little to make it easier to walk without having to duck under overhanging branches. We worked our way back to the pool and jumped in for a refreshing swim.

"You know, Eve, I wonder what sort of people could land on this island. If the movies are even partly accurate, pirates could be roaming around these waters. We should not reveal the entrance to the cavern. We will be outside most of the time, and will know if someone comes to rescue us. We should see them before they see us."

"Adam, I want to check something. I will stay here on the trail. Would you go stand just inside the entrance to the cave where you can see me?"

A few minutes later, I heard her say, "Yes, just as I thought. You are not visible from the trail, or even from the edge of the pool."

It was all bare rock between the edge of the pool and the entrance to the cave. All anyone could tell was that we made a trail to get fresh water. I felt a lot safer knowing that.

"Eve, I have read about people using leaves and straw for mattresses. Why don't we gather a bunch of leaves and make a place to sleep in the cavern? We can use the blanket to carry the leaves and then lay it on top when we are finished."

So we began searching for soft leaves to make our mattress. We included flower petals to make our bed smell good. In a few days, our cavern was beginning to feel like a home away from home.

One day I built a smoky fire in the cavern before climbing to the dome. Sure enough, we saw smoke coming from several places around the top of the mountain. The holes we found were just small cracks, but they let the smoke out, making it safe to have a fire if it got cold.

We began bringing dead wood to the cave to build a fire if needed.

"Eve, have you noticed that we can carry large bundles of firewood up the mountain and into our cave without stopping to rest several times, and neither of us is winded when we get here?"

"Yes, I feel like a new woman."

"Eve, I feel like I have stepped back in time at least twenty years. Four weeks of fresh fruit, clean air, and exercise have worked a miracle. I think we have a lot to be thankful for."

chapter eleven

The Storm

That evening, the air felt heavy. There was a strange stillness for about an hour. Then it started to rain. I thought that this could be a big storm. "Eve, we should close the doors of the plane and head for the cave."

We closed the doors and ran up the path. By the time we reached the pool, the wind was howling, and it was getting dark very fast. We felt our way into the cavern. Without the sun shining through the dome, it was very dark inside. I felt around and found the matches and lit a small fire for light.

The noise of the storm was awesome. The wind blowing across the vent holes was shrieking. About midnight, hail started to fall. It beat on the dome like a drum. It was well after 2:00 a.m. when we went to sleep from exhaustion. Neither of us got much sleep. In the morning, we got up and walked to the plane to evaluate the damage.

When we arrived, we were surprised to see what the wind had done. The plane had been moved up on the beach between the two trees it was tied to. That was not the strangest thing. The two trees had fallen to form a hedge in front of the plane, totally blocking it from view from the ocean.

After examining the plane, I determined that it was in perfect condition, and now it was only visible from the air.

chapter twelve

New Arrivals

Those trees are too large for us to move anytime soon. I don't feel like working hard today. Why don't we walk around the beach and see how the rest of the island looks after the storm?"

We walked all the way around to the north point in about an hour, and felt better than when we left.

We were just rounding the point when we spotted something white on the shore. It turned out to be sailcloth tied to a hollow tube. It looked like part of a sailboat. We decided to go up to the dome to find out if we could see more.

About forty-five minutes later, we were at the highest point, searching the water for signs of life, when I spotted a little dot of yellow several miles out. It looked like people paddling in a raft.

We walked back to the north point. By then we could see them from the shore. The wind was usually out of the west, but that day it was out of the northeast, as if God was bringing them to us. There is a sand bar that runs out several hundred feet from both points of our island. I walked out about 150 feet and waited.

Soon they were close enough for me to talk to them. I asked, “do you have a rope?” The woman said, “Yes.” The man looked like he would collapse at any moment. “Can you throw me the end of the rope?” I asked. I told them to stop paddling and rest. I towed them around the point and into the cove.

Eve and I pulled them up near the plane. When we beached their raft, they got out and we carried the raft up into the shade of the trees.

From where we sat, they could see the plane. The man pleaded, “Would you help us get back to the mainland?” I replied, “We could if we had gas and electrical power. We were stranded here late October. This island saved our lives in more than one way. We will tell you our story later, but what happened to you, and who are you?”

chapter thirteen

PIRATES

The man said, "Honey, why don't you tell them while I rest a bit?"

"OK, Rob. I am June, and this is my husband, Rob. We retired in July for health reasons. The doctors gave me up as a hopeless case. I have bone cancer, and their treatments only seemed to make me worse. Rob has a bad back and cannot work any longer.

"We decided to go on a sailing trip to enjoy the last year of our life together. We had been sailing from port to port for about two months. Last night, we were out enjoying the sun and the sweet breeze when pirates slipped up beside our sailboat.

"They pointed guns at us and boarded our boat. They stole all our valuables and food. They then took all our sails and threw them overboard. Just before they left, they disabled our engine. They only left our life raft. They even broke our compass.

"With no way to control the boat, it went down in the storm last night. We held on to our life raft and just drifted with the storm until morning. At sunrise, we spotted the top of your island. Rob did most of the paddling since then, using the only paddle we had."

"It sounds like you endured quite an ordeal. I am Adam Westbrook, and this is my wife, Eve. We believe God brought us here for a purpose last month, after leaving the U.S. for a short vacation. We both were diagnosed with cancer. I had blocked arteries and prostate cancer. Eve had breast cancer, diabetes and arthritis. We were both scheduled for surgery three weeks ago.

"We believe if we had accepted the surgery and treatments, we would be dead right now. God intervened. We now feel better than we have in years. Do you know the Lord?"

Rob spoke up, "Yes, we are Christians, but I am sorry to say we have not been too close to the Lord for some time. I guess I have been angry that He was taking June from me."

Eve jumped into the conversation, "It will be dark soon. Now that you have had a few minutes to catch your breath, are you up for a walk? We will gather our meal as we go."

I asked Rob to help me hide the raft. We placed it beside the plane. I noticed a suitcase and a bundle of things in a pillowcase. "Let's take your things." We helped them up to the pool. "If you want, you can wash off the salt water." We gave them fruit, and I started a fire in the cave while Eve helped them into the water. They gently swam around a few minutes and Eve helped them climb out.

By then, I was back. As the sun was setting, we entered the cave by the light from the fire inside. Rob asked, "How have you survived here for six weeks, Adam?"

"Well, as we were leaving the U.S., our daughter gave us some information on health. In those two small books, we found that God designed our bodies to be nourished by raw fruit and vegetables. We learned that disease develops when you eat too much cooked food and not enough raw. You see, our bodies are self-healing if we give them the tools they need. We need living enzymes from living food to feed our living bodies.

"We had an abundance of raw fruit and plants to eat, so we decided not to try fishing. As you may have noticed, there are no animals on the island. We only use the fire for light and heat. We were both overweight and sick. Now we feel better than when we were married thirty-five years ago. I know we are stronger.

"Well, folks, it is getting late. Why don't you sleep in our bed over there and we will sleep in our plane. In the morning, we will bring you breakfast and figure out what to do next. Before we leave, I would like to pray with you:

"Father God, Master of the universe, we thank You for bringing our new friends, Rob and June, safely through the storm. We believe You had a purpose when You brought us to this island. We also believe You had a purpose in bringing Rob and June here to join us.

"Father, none of us has any idea where we are in this world but I believe we are in the center of Your will for us. Father, we pray that You give Rob and June the peace You have given us and that You will heal their bodies and hearts as You have ours.

"We thank You for these new friends to share our lives with. We trust we will have many hours of sweet fellowship. As we all adjust, Father, help us to be patient, supportive, loving, and kind with each other. Help us to work together as a team, as a family, and as brothers and sisters in Christ. Amen."

Eve and I left the cave and went to the plane. We were very happy to have the opportunity to help Rob and June. We experienced a very contented sleep.

chapter fourteen

Exploring

In the morning, we went back up to the cave. Rob and June were just getting up.

"Did you two sleep well?"

"Surprisingly so. Thank you, Adam, we did."

"Eve and I have been up for a couple hours talking about what to do next. We have only explored part of the island. Most of the last six weeks have been spent setting up camp. We need to help you find a place of your own or divide the cave for privacy.

"This island is quite small. If we explore a little first, we may find other caves or sheltered spots that would be suitable for a place for you.

"If there are other caves, they would have to be on the other end of the island or below where we are now. Based on the shape of this cavern and its dome, I am sure it takes up most of this end of the mountain. We have not explored the entire cavern nor most of the north end of the island. To make it easy for you this first day, perhaps we should explore the cavern a little better. If you are up to it, we can start exploring outside tomorrow."

So I led the way into the cavern and back toward the north wall. We had not been up close to the wall to see if there were any small caves there. I must have been looking down and ahead of us because I was surprised when Rob called out, "Adam, look up there." He was pointing up to a shelf-like area.

We climbed up with some difficulty and found a large flat slab of rock about ten feet in diameter, which was leaning against the wall. It was very dark behind the slab, but it looked like an opening.

In the trinkets we had purchased on our way to the island were some candles inside glass tube stands. I had been saving them for such a day. I lit one of them and handed it to Rob. "You found it. You lead the way." Rob led, and the four of us squeezed into the opening one at a time.

This cave was narrow and soon dropped at about a forty-five degree angle. We moved slowly as not to blow out our candle. It dropped about one hundred feet and then turned northwest. We smelled fresh air coming from around the corner and saw light coming from ahead. Another sharp turn to the east, and we faced the opening.

We stepped out into the light onto a large slab of smooth, flat rock. It was not visible from the mountain because trees engulfed it. I said, "Definitely not living quarters, but a great secret escape route.

"Rob, you said pirates attacked your boat. If we saw them, we could get into our cavern and out the back way. I don't think they would search long enough to find this secret tunnel."

"Adam, I think you are right. We can carry our knives and your hand ax all the time, so even if they take or destroy our comforts, we will be safe. We can always rebuild our beds and anything else we make."

"Right. Also, this is a shortcut to explore the east side of the island for food."

"Adam, I agree to a point. But we should not use it enough to create a path to the tunnel entrance. We know the sides of the tunnel are smooth and there are no trip hazards. We could enter and move down without light. We should explore the immediate area now and not use the tunnel unless it is an emergency."

"Girls, do you agree that we should not use this shortcut to protect its secrecy?"

"Yes," they said in unison. June added, "I am not tired, and since the east beach must be nearby, let's not even go back that way. We have all day, why don't we see what we can find here and work our way back to the cave?"

We were still on the flat rock when Eve let out a scream of delight. "Look, Adam, is that what I think it is?" We looked, and I jumped down to pick up a volleyball-sized watermelon. I tossed it up to Rob and climbed back on the rock slab.

"Well, folks," I said, "are you ready for a mid-morning treat?" We sat down to taste the watermelon, and it was the best I had ever eaten.

In a moment of silence while we ate, I could clearly hear the surf. "The beach must be very close," I remarked. It was my guess that it was less than a hundred yards away.

chapter fifteen

A Home for Rob and June

When we finished the watermelon, Rob spoke, "Adam, Eve, this spot would make a really nice floor to a roundhouse. If we don't find anything better by tomorrow, why don't we build a house right here? That way, June and I can watch over the east side and you can watch over the west side. If either of us sees any sign of pirates, we can go through the secret tunnel to warn the others. We could build it against the mountain and hide the entrance to the tunnel with something.

"We can walk around the long way everyday to get together. Also, that way we can watch both sides for signs of rescuers. We can describe the pirate ship for you so you can tell it apart from a rescue vessel."

We walked straight out from the mountain and, sure enough, the tree line was only about one hundred feet wide. It would be simple to clear a path if we built a home for Rob and June on this spot.

I confirmed that we were closer to the north end of the island. We explored between the base of the mountain and the beach, all the way to the north point. We stopped several times so Rob and June could rest. We found many new fruits and vegetables, but no sign of a cave.

Later, as we were walking by the plane, Rob pointed out, "You know, Adam, if the pirates came here, they would most likely destroy that plane or tow it away. We should camouflage it really well and stay away from it so they would hopefully miss it. They may just follow the trail to the pool."

"Rob, you are probably right. There are several vines clinging to the top of the standing trees that are still connected to these that fell down. I don't know what kind of trees they are, but they seem to be alive with half of their roots up in the air. If we brought in some other limbs to form a dense hedge type fence, and transplanted some of the fast growing vines, it would soon be well hidden.

"Yes, if we do it right, in a few weeks it will look like part of the jungle. We must be well off the beaten path. Eve and I have not seen any kind of aircraft flying over since we arrived.

"Rob, you look beat. June, you don't look much better. Let's take a swim and relax the rest of the day. We can talk more about our experiences here on the island, and make plans."

We picked some bananas on the way to the pool. Eve said, "This is how we wash our clothes." She stepped up to the stone lip of the pool and jumped in. "With the afternoon sun beating down, you will be dry in an hour or so." We all jumped in, swam around a bit, and climbed up on the rocks to soak up the sun.

As we lay there sunbathing, I elaborated on my retirement, the doctor's prognosis, and how our children agreed that we take a vacation, as it would most likely be our last one, ever.

I told them what we learned from the books on health and what to expect in the next few days. I said, "I believe God brought you here for your health. I believe your work for Him is not finished. I don't know what we will face before someone comes to take us off this island, but I do know that God never makes a mistake."

Rob added, "June and I talked last night and we feel the same. We think God brought us together for a purpose. We will just have to trust God to guide us."

I proposed, "With that settled, I think your idea of hiding the plane is what we should do tomorrow before exploring or building a house. I have another bright idea. Those trees that hide the front of the plane have shallow roots. There are two more behind the plane. The ropes are no longer needed to hold the plane. If we tie them together, and I climb up to tie the rope close to the top, we may be able to pull the trees over so they help hide the sides as well."

Rob said, "That is a crazy idea but it might just work. If it does, we will only have a few holes to fill. We should be able to make it look like a naturally thick section of underbrush."

"OK, I expect that you and June will have a healing crisis within the next few days. If we have no trouble tipping the trees over it will take about one day per side. Exploring the rest of the island could take another three or four days. I think the best plan is to hide the plane, and then build some screens from palm leaves and bamboo to make two bedrooms in the cavern. Later, if we build your house on the east side of the mountain and we have a big storm, you may want to come into the cavern with us. If your room is in the back by the escape tunnel, it will provide safety and privacy at the same time. What do you think?"

"I think it is a great plan. It will be our first home on the island."

chapter sixteen

Hiding the Plane

The last time I had climbed a tree, I was about ten years old. The hard part was getting to the first branch. I was glad I had not tried it six weeks earlier. I doubt that I would have survived. As it was, I had very little trouble going up, but coming down was a bit scarier. I lost my footing and slipped a few times. Fortunately, I had a good hold of a branch each time and made it down safely. We pulled on the rope and the tree did not budge.

Next, we dug around and cut the roots on the side, away from the direction we were trying to make it fall, and pulled again. It wiggled a little but that was all. I remembered the principle of a pulley and tied the loose end of the rope to another tree as far away as I could. Then all four of us pulled the rope sideways. As soon as we put our weight on the rope, the tree started to move. We pulled as hard as we could and, with the help of the wind, the tree moved. We kept pulling perpendicular to the direction the tree was falling, and were safely out of the way when it hit the ground.

That left us a small gap on either side. To fill it in, we transplanted small trees and vines from the sides of the trail that goes to the pool. It turned out to be a long, hard day but we were pleased with our work. In a very short time, anyone following our trail would not be able to see the plane.

The next day, Rob had severe cold symptoms and stayed in bed. June supplied him with water, and the three of us worked on bringing in palm fronds and bamboo to build the screens and another bed. While gathering the leaves, we found that we could take stringy fibers from some of the leaves to tie the bamboo into a framework. We were then able to weave the palm fronds into screens that would hide our beds and allow a person to dress in privacy.

By the end of that day we had the original bed enclosed and the framework for the second enclosure in place. We also had most of the leaves we would need inside.

The next morning, June had a fever and Rob was still sick. Eve and I provided for their comfort the best we could and worked on the other enclosure. By the time we finished the enclosure and the bed made out of leaves, which we covered with the sailcloth, Rob was feeling a little better. We gave him the books on health and suggested that he sit by the pool and read. He agreed and did just that.

It was still several hours before night. We told June and Rob that we were going for a walk. We stopped at the watermelon patch and picked two nice melons. On the way back to camp, we talked about all the recent events and enjoyed each other's company. As we rounded the north point, I asked Eve, "Do you know that tomorrow is Sunday?" She nodded.

"Now that it is not just the two of us, we should have some kind of worship service. Rob and June need the rest anyway. When we were alone, we rested on Sunday, but I feel so blessed that I think we should do more."

"I agree. I am sure we all know enough songs by heart to sing. Couldn't you pray and give us a message?"

"I will definitely pray about that and ask God to lead. If June is not up to going outside, we can do it by her bed."

When we approached the pool, Rob looked up from the book he was reading. "My doctor never told me any of this stuff. If all of this is true, it is a wonder that we have lived this long."

"You are right there. I don't know for sure, but I think the lump in my breast is getting much smaller. The pain in Adam's prostate is gone. We both feel younger."

"We were just talking about starting worship services and resting on Sunday. Tomorrow is Sunday. What do you think?"

"Adam, it is a wonderful idea. Would you do me a favor? Let me tell June. She really likes good surprises and will be thrilled."

"Then she should enjoy hearing something that we did not tell you before we left. We finished your bed."

We went in and found her burning up with fever. She was sweating profusely. I said, "I think the fever will break soon. Let's carry her over to your bed and she can use our blanket; that should help. The stream is close if she needs water. We will use the good clothes that we don't need here to cover our bed, and we will stay close in case you need us tonight."

chapter seventeen

Church

It was almost noon when Rob and June woke up. Rob said June's fever broke at about 2 a.m. He then was able to go to sleep. We had placed the watermelon in the stream. It was cool. We sliced off small pieces for them and they were delighted with the taste.

Rob then told June about our plans for Sunday. She was very happy. We sang "Amazing Grace," "Victory in Jesus," "Because He Lives," and other songs.

"I did not tell you many things about our lives before we came here," I said.

"I felt called to preach many years ago. At that time, God did not see fit to give me a flock. I believe it is now my time. I have prayed about it, and if you are willing, I feel that God wants me to assume spiritual leadership over our small flock of four."

"Adam, June and I have trusted your leadership role for our physical survival. So, yes, we welcome you as our spiritual leader as well."

"Thank you for your confidence. I hope I will live up to it. Let's pray:

"Father God, in the name of Jesus, we come to You asking for complete peace in the matter of my assuming the role of spiritual head of our small group. I don't feel that I am worthy. However, Father, I know You make no mistakes. We ask for Your hand to be upon all of us. We ask Lord, that You help us grow so close to You that we can hear Your still small voice when You speak to us.

"From all we can see, we know that You have provided a little piece of paradise for us. Though we don't have many of the creature comforts we once had, we have all our needs met, which you have promised to supply. We thank You, Father, for keeping Your promises.

"You have promised to protect us, Father. We have done nearly all in our power to protect ourselves from pirates. This cavern, which You provided, protects us from the storms, but we have no weapons to fight off determined pirates. Lord God, we place ourselves in Your hand of protection. We trust that You will keep us safe. We trust that, when You are ready, You will provide a way for us to return home to our families.

"Father, it appears that You brought us here to heal our diseases. We thank You for Your marvelous grace and mercy to us. We don't know what Your ultimate plan is, but we trust You to reveal that plan to us, as we are ready to receive it.

"Father, we are thankful beyond words. All I can say, Lord, is thank You, thank You, thank You. Amen."

"Amen," rang out the others.

"I will not be preaching to you today. It is the thanksgiving season. I think we will just each express our thanks to God for His provision and sing some more."

I started, "I am thankful for two new friends to share our island with. I am sorry that you were attacked by pirates and that you lost your boat, but thankful that you did not die and that God saw fit to bring you here."

Eve was next. "I am thankful that our daughter gave us the books on health that now mean so much to us. I also am thankful that our dear Creator saved Rob and June from the pirates and the storm, and brought them to us. Praise God from whom all blessings flow."

June followed, "I am thankful for this little piece of paradise and for new friends who traveled ahead of us, who are willing to guide us back to health. Only God could have done this."

Rob concluded the session, "I am so thankful to God for bringing us this knowledge. Though I am tired, I already feel a reduction in the pain. I have no more painkillers left, but I feel less discomfort. I am thankful for Adam and Eve's hospitality. I praise God for bringing us together for this great adventure."

"Amen," we all added.

We sang for a while and rested all day. Rob and June read the books on health. Eve and I read our Bibles. That evening, we prayed together and got the best sleep since our arrival.

Monday, we all got up ready to face any challenge. We wanted to get the plane out of hiding some day, but in the meantime, we made it look as much like virgin landscape as possible. Our hope was that if pirates found the island, they would follow the path and miss the plane.

Since everyone felt like exploring, we went to the south point, spread out, and worked our way through the jungle all the way up to the flat rock, staying close to the beach. Late that morning, we enjoyed some watermelon and rested.

On the way back, we stayed close to the mountain. We were about halfway to the south point when we found a dense area of vines. On closer investigation, we discovered that they were kiwi vines. The fruit was still very green and small. It would start getting ripe in a few weeks.

We continued through the trees along the mountain. We discovered more flowers and an abundance of banana and coconut, but no caves.

Since we were tired and sweating, we went for a swim, had a leisurely meal, and talked about the abundance of food. We figured that the island could support fifty to one hundred people, depending on the season. I wondered whether any country had claimed this island. Until we were rescued, there was no way to know.

chapter eighteen

Discovery

We continued our exploration of the island the following day. We spread out as we did the day before and went north, close to the edge of the trees along the beach. We came back along the mountain. I was just below the tree line on the side of the mountain. Rob was just below me. Eve was working her way along the base. June was following where it was easier to walk.

Suddenly, I heard a crash. I looked down and … no Rob. I called out, and Eve came into view. I started going down when I found a hole about the size of a manhole cover. I could see Rob about eight feet down. He was not moving.

Eve was coming up to meet me. I told her to watch her step. I gingerly moved around the hole. It looked like I could push on the lower lip of the hole to make the rock fall away and enter safely. I asked Eve to move over, and just then saw June coming. I told her Rob fell into a hole. "I am going to try to make the hole bigger so I can get in. I need you to move over by Eve so any falling rock doesn't hurt you."

I got into position and pushed with my feet on the sharp top edge. A large thin slab fell away, revealing the mouth of a cave. I quickly got down and went to Rob. He had a gash on the back of his head but he was breathing. I put pressure on the wound and talked to him to see if I could wake him.

I released the wound and noticed the blood flow had slowed. I grabbed him under the arms and pulled him out of the cave. "We will have to get him back to the cavern where we have first-aid supplies. I am going to carry him over my shoulder. Eve, I need you to lead the way and look for hazards that could trip me. June, I need you to hold his head and keep pressure on that wound."

I made it as far as the edge of the pool. My legs were about to give out. I said, "I am going to have to lay him down here. Eve, would you go in and get the first-aid supplies? We have more light here anyway. June, would you get some water from the stream so we can start cleaning this wound? It may be a blessing if he does not wake up right away."

We had a couple of towels hanging on the bushes. June soaked them with water. We cleaned up the wound so we could see it well by the time Eve returned. Eve stitched up the wound after placing some disinfectant on it.

About a half-hour later, Rob started moaning and soon woke up. "Don't move quickly," I warned. He just lay there a few minutes. I inquired, "Can you move your arms and legs?" He was able to move everything, so I asked him whether he wanted to try sitting up. I placed my hand behind his back and helped him into a sitting position. I advised him, "Just sit there a few minutes before you try to stand."

"What happened?" Rob wondered.

"You fell into a cave and you hit your head on a sharp rock. You suffered a big gash on the back of your head. I was able to enlarge the cave opening and get you out. I carried you here and we cleaned, stitched, and dressed your wound. How do you feel?"

“A little dizzy still, but OK.”

I asked him whether he was up to eating lunch, and he responded, “Yes. Adam, and I think I will be ready to explore that cave in an hour or so.”

“Rob, are you sure? Asked June. Don’t get all macho on us. If you are not up to this, we can wait until tomorrow.”

“I’m fine. Let’s walk in that direction. If I feel any problems, I will say so and we can come back.”

We brought matches and a candle and went back to our discovery. We went in, and it quickly opened up into a room about thirty feet in diameter. “This would make a very nice home for us,” said Rob. June agreed.

I told everyone, “We need to be very careful when we walk around. There may be other hidden caves with fragile openings, like this one. None of us should ever explore alone. If you had been by yourself, most likely, we would not have found you until it was too late.

“Can we all agree on that? Our mountain may be honeycombed with small caves like this, possibly hundreds of them. Perhaps if we carried a stick and tapped the ground, we could hear a hollow sound that would warn us of a cave.” Everyone agreed.

“It seems that the steam from the spring did to the lava that formed this island what yeast does to bread. If I am right, we have a thin crust and a lot of holes. It is getting late. We should go back to the main camp and discuss our options.”

Back by the pool, I prayed:

“Father God, we praise You for Your hand of protection. We thank You because Rob only had a cut on his head with apparently no lasting injury. Lord, we don’t know what You have in store for us here.

We ask that You guide us into the correct decisions as to where Rob and June should set up housekeeping. Amen.

"We have no way to know what dangers we may face from pirates or storms. The new cave is close to our main cave and requires less work to make it livable. On the other hand, if people lived on the other side of the mountain, they could give us early warning of friend or foe.

"Another thought I have is this: we have no clear idea of what God is planning for us. All we know is that He has brought us here. I am convinced the information on God's plan for health we brought with us, along with this new lifestyle, is healing our bodies. God could bring others here to join us before He provides us with a way off this island.

"All we can do is thank God for each new day and see what it brings. But has any of you thought about the prospect of living out our lives here? Who knows how many others could end up joining us here? Look at the sky. It looks like another storm is coming."

chapter nineteen

Another Storm, New Friends

That night, another storm hit. It howled as loud as the last one. At sunrise, we went out to survey the damage. Just in case, we climbed to the top of the dome and scanned the horizon. In the same general area where we first saw Rob and June, we saw a large yellow dot bouncing on the waves.

About noon, we spotted four people in a raft. Soon, we could see a second raft. Again, we met them at the point. Again, we suggested that they just lay there while we towed them up close to the trail. With four of us pulling the ropes, we had them on the beach in about twenty minutes.

"Hi friends, welcome to our island. Let's carry your rafts up to the shade."

We sat down and I addressed them, "Who are you? What brings you here?"

The older of the men spoke up. "This is Jim Blackman and his wife Sarah, and this is my wife Mary. My name is John Green. Jim is a mining engineer. He lost his job two weeks ago and wanted a little adventure. He has advanced arthritis, in his back and knees, and could not handle the demanding work in the mines. His dear wife, Sarah, was diagnosed last week with cancer in her uterus. She is scheduled to have surgery the first week of January. Mary was told last month that she has an inoperable brain tumor. Our children are all out of the house. The four of us have been friends for a long time. I am a carpenter. I have arthritis in my back, hands and shoulders. It is getting very hard for me to work. It is the slow season for me, so we decided to take a vacation.

"Yesterday, before the storm, pirates boarded our boat and stole all our money, credit cards, jewelry, food, water, and the engine of our boat. While they were removing the engine, they busted a huge hole in the hull, larger than we could ever hope to fix, just above the water line. We were sinking.

"I don't know why, but I had some of my basic hand-powered carpenter tools, and other supplies hidden in the boat. We had two life rafts and the storm was coming. So we loaded everything the pirates overlooked into the second raft, covered it with sailcloth, and tied it down. We tied the two rafts together and got in just before our boat sank. Then the storm brought us here. Where are we?"

I admitted, "We are not sure where we are. However, we know that we are in the center of God's will, and that He has brought you here for a purpose. What do you have beside the sailcloth and carpenter tools in your raft?"

"I have no idea why we brought so much, but we have a lot of extra clothes, two dozen blankets, three dozen sets of sheets and pillowcases. We also have many towels, washcloths, and a large first-aid kit. Besides the normal saws and hammers, I have hand planes, draw knives and an assortment of chisels, a good ax, and two shovels. I guess we were expecting to travel around the islands helping any needy people we could find."

In unison, the four of us cheered, "Praise God."

I said, "I suppose you would like to rinse the salt water off. You are most likely hungry." They nodded, and I said, "I thought so. Before we continue the introductions, are you up for a short walk?"

They said, "Yes." I guided them to the pool. We picked some bananas along the path. When we reached the pool, Eve repeated her little speech, "This is how we wash our clothes," as she jumped in the water with her clothes on.

While we all ate bananas, I narrated my arrival with Eve, the pirate attack on Rob and June, and the fact that we all had left the U.S. for the same reason: our health.

I told them that Eve and I had arrived with nothing but a meager supply of clothes, our small survival kit, and the books on health. But I Praised God about how, after only twelve weeks, virtually all our symptoms were gone.

Furthermore, Rob acknowledged that he and June had nearly recovered from all their symptoms, and he felt that God had brought us all together for a purpose. They heard that, just a week earlier, Rob had fallen into a hidden cave. How we were able to rescue him and his quick recovery.

Then I commented, "From your description of the events before the storm, I think we are quite some distance out in the ocean. I am afraid the pirates are patrolling the waters between the mainland and us. We must be outside the normal shipping lanes and flight routes. We can be sure that if we went east, we could find land. My guess is that the pirates stay within sixty miles of the mainland and the Virgin Islands. We must be at least thirty miles beyond the pirates' territory. Therefore, my estimate is that we are about three hundred to four hundred miles southwest of St. Thomas.

"With the currents moving northeast, and the prevailing wind out of the west, I don't think we stand a chance of paddling to the mainland, past the pirates, and surviving. We have everything we need right here. I believe God brought us together for a purpose. With your arrival, I am convinced, more than ever, that God is assembling a team for some great work.

"Every one of us left the U.S. because of a health issue. But look at my wife, Eve. Twelve weeks ago, she was bent over with arthritis. Her diabetes was getting worse. They were about to take her off the pills and put her on insulin shots. She had breast cancer. There was a painful lump in her left breast. Her doctor did not give us much hope that she would survive the surgery and treatment.

"Now she walks erect, without pain. She has been completely off all her medication for over six weeks. She has no pain in her breast and cannot feel the lump that was there. Her skin is no longer wrinkled. If I did not know differently, I would say she was forty, not sixty.

"Twelve weeks ago, I could not walk ten minutes without stopping for a breather. The pain in my chest just would not allow it. A few days ago, when Rob fell into the mouth of a hidden cave and was knocked unconscious, I carried him about 300 yards, through the jungle, and up to this spot without stopping. When I laid him down, though my legs were at the end of their endurance, I was not out of breath. I was able to go right to work cleaning his wound so that Eve could disinfect and stitch it.

"We wanted to build a dwelling on the east side of the island, but all we had was a hand ax and a knife and no knowledge of construction. We find that we may have many small caves that could be used for dwellings, but they are hidden and dangerous to find. So what does the next storm bring us? A carpenter with tools and a mining engineer! I just cannot believe that is an accident. With the knowledge we have gained, I am convinced we can guide you back to health. With your training and skill, we can create many safe dwellings that preserve our island's ability to produce the food we need to survive. In my opinion, this was not an accident. It was the hand of God.

"In case you have not figured it out, the others have allowed me to assume physical and spiritual leadership. I hope you will do likewise, at least for the time being. Perhaps in a month or two, if you are not happy, we can vote on both roles. It is getting late. We need to get your supply raft out of sight and make beds for you. I have an idea: your life raft turned upside down may serve as a bed, at least for tonight. It should fit through the mouth of the cavern. We will give up our bed to one couple for the night and sleep in our plane, which we will show you tomorrow."

We went back to the beach and, with all of us lifting, were able to easily move the supply raft with all the contents intact. We carried it up to the pool so that it was not visible from the beach. We took the other raft into the cavern and picked a good place to turn it upside down. It was like a rubber hammock. "I am sure that will be more comfortable than the ground."

It was growing dark, so we built a fire. We gathered around the fire and I suggested holding hands and praying:

"Father God, in the name of Jesus Christ, our Savior, we come before You as a united group. Father, we see Your hand in everything that is happening here. We praise You and thank You for the blessing of our new friends who have joined us today. We thank You for our healing and trust that You will do the same for our new friends.

"Father, I am beginning to see a vision of a very unique place where people can come to regain health. I don't know if You will just keep bringing more people here, or if You will provide a way for us to take those who want to leave back to the mainland.

"Father, Eve and I have become so content in our simple life here that we would like to spend our remaining days here helping others. We do feel a strong desire to let our families know that we are OK and where we are. But Father, we trust that You will care for that in Your time as well.

"Father, You are providing everything we need to build a great work through You in this place. Help us always to give You the honor and praise You deserve. Thank You for Your infinite wisdom and grace. Amen and Hallelujah."

chapter twenty

More Discoveries

After greeting the others in the morning, I proceeded to discuss the plans for the day. "Now that our group is growing, we need to do some planning. I want to start some projects with Jim and John. First, we need to get these supplies inside the cavern and see what you brought." Jim agreed, "That sounds like a plan." So we untied the sailcloth and started carrying in the supplies.

Rob was walking behind me. I grabbed an armload of blankets and stood up. He let fly a loud "Praise the Lord." I looked down and saw four Coleman lanterns. As John approached me, I asked, "How much fuel did you bring for the lanterns?" He replied, "We have five gallons. We also have five gross of candles and a dozen candleholders with grass chimneys."

Rob asked, "How did the pirates miss all this?"

John explained, "That is an interesting story. We purchased this boat from an auction of drug runners' boats and planes. There was a large cargo compartment behind a concealed door in the bow once used for smuggling drugs. They took everything in sight but never investigated further. There are a few more surprises you will like: a surveyor's transit and climbing equipment, as well as many kinds of anchor bolts with nuts and star drills to make holes for the bolts. We also have two miles of electric fence wire that would be handy for tying things together. We also brought an assortment of wood screws. One more thing, we have a guitar. Mary plays the guitar."

All I could say was, "God is so good."

We soon had all the supplies inside. I wanted to show them the plane. As we approached the beach, I instructed them to follow me without disturbing anything. We were trying not to make any marks that would show the pirates where the plane was. We went through the trees and brush to the backside of the enclosure. Stepping through the last wall of brush, they gasped, "That is a beautiful plane. You say all it needs is fuel and the electrical problem fixed."

"Wow", said Jim, "Now we know we need to pray for a barrel of gas and an aircraft mechanic."

John commented, "You say these trees fell in a storm and missed the plane. This is a miracle."

I clarified, "Two of them did. We pulled this one over to help hide the plane."

"Look at this," declared Jim, "it looks like these treetops are taking root and are growing. This new growth may not need the old roots any longer. I wonder whether we could design a hangar by cutting the trunk off this one on the north and making a movable gate to take the plane in and out."

Rob had a proposal, "There is an easy way to test your theory. There are a lot of small trees like this one. We can knock over a small one, see if it takes root like these did, cut the trunk off, and see if it keeps growing. If it continues to live, we can assume that the same will happen with this one."

I had to interrupt the animated conversation as it was getting late. "There is a lot to do today. What would you like for lunch? Close by, we have bananas, coconut, oranges, and an unknown fruit."

Since John wanted to see the mystery fruit, we took a short walk through the jungle and picked enough for a meal. We found a convenient place to sit and ate our lunch. John studied the fruit. "I have seen pictures of these but can't recall the name. All I remember is that they are too fragile to ship, that is why we don't see them in stores. They sure do taste good."

After we ate, I told them, "In case you were wondering why I brought this lantern, we are about halfway between the cave that Rob found the hard way and the cavern. I have a suspicion I want to confirm.

"Eve, would you take the ladies up to the cavern and work on making things a little more comfortable for tonight? I would like you to keep an eye on the back wall of the cavern. Let us know if you see light. We will go up to the new cave and have a good look."

The men followed me to the cave Rob found. We lit the lantern and went in. "Jim, it looks like either steam or gas bubbles formed this cave and the main cavern, much like a glass blower forms a drinking glass or pitcher. I am sure you noticed the light coming in from the roof of the cavern. We won't walk up there today, but at the top of the mountain, there is a smooth dome that resembles a large lens for sunglasses, like a dark window. That is why I thought that perhaps the wall between this cave and the cavern might be thin enough to let light through."

Jim nodded, "Yes, Adam, I think you are correct. A small cave like this would only need a small amount of steam to create it. I agree with you, it is likely that more of these caves are hidden in this mountain. I could safely find them. The steam bubble theory would also explain the relatively smooth walls of all the caves. This rock looks very brittle, almost like glass. We could level a section of floor to make comfortable living quarters here."

I said, "OK, let's go back to the main cavern and see what the girls are up to."

When we walked in, we did not have to ask. June cried out, "We saw a dull glow right over there on the wall! Did you hear us yelling?"

"No, we did not hear you, but your sight of the light confirms the crystalline nature of the rock. That is why the sunlight comes in through the dome. I want to test something. You two look quite tired. Why don't you sit here and rest? I will be back within twenty minutes. Rob, would you come with me, please? Jim, John, in case you are wondering, we decided to go out in pairs after Rob fell into the cave and got hurt." We went back to the little cave and left a lantern sitting there.

When we returned, we could see the glow on the wall. Rob exclaimed, "I think I figured out what you are thinking: that it might be close to the tunnel!"

John and Jim inquired in unison, "What tunnel?"

I explained, "We were going to show you that next. Do you girls feel up to rock climbing yet?"

Mary moaned, "I don't. In fact, I don't feel good at all."

I realized she needed more rest and said, "OK, we will be back in an hour or so. Men, we have a short climb and then about ten minutes walking. Are you ready?"

We grabbed another lantern and climbed the back wall up to the escape tunnel. I did not light the lantern. When we entered the tunnel, we saw what I suspected: a bright glow coming from the small cave! "Jim, it looks like the back wall of the cave is very close to this tunnel. Would your star drills cut through this rock? We may be able to make an emergency exit for the small cave."

Jim answered, "Yes, they will. When do you want me to start?"

"We will discuss that when we get back. I did not fill the lantern I left in the cave so it will burn out quickly. Rob, why don't you lead the way?" I handed him the lantern, which we lit, and we walked down to the flat rock.

When we were out of the tunnel, I asked, "John, wouldn't this make a nice floor for a house? Also, if we build it here, wouldn't it be easy to hide the tunnel entrance?"

"Yes on both counts, " he answered.

I described the plan. "What we had in mind was to build a house that could be seen through an opening to the beach. One couple could watch this side of the island and warn us of danger, and we could do the same without being seen. If pirates came here, they could destroy the house but its residents would be safe. We have an abundance of building material as you can see: trees, bamboo, and much more.

"Anyway, this gives us a lot to discuss. It is getting late in the afternoon. I am sure you two are getting tired. Rob, let's both grab a couple of watermelons." We jumped off the rock and each got hold of two nice ones. "OK, let's go back up the tunnel and join the girls." About fifteen minutes later, we were all in the main cavern sitting around a small fire.

I initiated a discussion on various issues. "First, I want to tell you a little about an effective health plan. The books our daughter sent with us teach that our bodies were designed for a diet of raw fruit and vegetables, with some nuts and seeds. As it turns out, fruit, vegetables, and coconut are the only food on the island. We could find fish but, so far, no one has brought any fishing gear. Our health has improved so much that we have not been inclined to go fishing.

"You need to know what to expect. It looks like Mary is already showing signs of a healing crisis. All of us had at least one. When you return to the original diet and lifestyle God designed for us, your body will begin to clean house. You may experience a variety of symptoms. They can range from the flu, the common cold, diarrhea, high fever, or a combination. For the four of us, our first healing crisis was within a few days of arrival. When you are in the middle of a healing crisis, according to the books, it is best to just rest, drink water, and eat juicy fruit only if you are hungry. None of us were hungry while going through our first healing crisis.

"Your body does most of its cleansing while you sleep. Because of that, we have found that you will most likely feel it first when you try to get up in the morning.

"OK, enough for now. You can read the books. I want to do some planning. There are enough of us now, so we can work on more than one project at a time. I like our spirit of community, but I don't want a commune. Can we all agree that the simplest project would be to create a home in the small cave?"

Jim agreed, "Yes, we could quickly make a level floor."

John volunteered, "I could build a platform with legs on the low side. It would not take up room on the floor. Also, we could make bamboo shelves for clothes, blankets, and the like."

Jim suggested, "While you are in there fixing up the room, I can go into the tunnel and see about cutting a back door."

I had noticed a small drafting kit and paper with the supplies. "Jim, in your spare time, could you draw a map of the island and show the relationship between the big cavern and the small cave, the escape tunnel and the flat rock? There is no hurry, but if we have more guests in the future, we could show them the map.

"You two look like kids in a candy store."

"Well, Adam, you would think that being stranded on a small island would be devastating, but we are having the time of our lives. To us, this is a great adventure. We are excited about the future and look forward to what God has in store for us. The simple life you have been living sounds wonderful after the hectic lives we left back home. The prospect of having our physical problems just disappear is very encouraging as well. Your testimonies give us hope of a bright future."

We prayed, and I thanked God for how we seemed to fit together as a team and for His many blessings. We were excited, but we needed our sleep for the next busy day. So Eve and I retired back to the plane.

"Adam, I feel so blessed. God brought us such wonderful people. I would like to be able to contact our families, but I would like to stay here 'til God calls us home."

"My dear Eve, I feel the same. I wake up each morning expecting a blessing. I never felt so at home with so little. All we can do is take one day at a time. I don't know how to express the joy and peace I feel. It is just awesome."

chapter twenty-one

A Home for Jim and Sarah

The next morning we went into the cavern. Mary was coughing and moaning due to severe sinus congestion and other cold symptoms. Sarah was not feeling well either. Knowing that they could not do anything and that they needed rest, I asked Eve and June to stay with them. I asked Jim to see about cutting a hole between the tunnel and the cave. "John, if you are feeling OK, I would like you to come with Rob and myself. We will get started on the work at the cave. What should we bring?"

He said, "I will bring my tools. You and Rob can bring the ax, sledgehammer, shovels, a spool of wire, a gallon of gas for the lantern, and those five-gallon buckets." We picked up our tools and marched out to the cave. There was a lot of bamboo along the base of the mountain, close to the cave, along the trail we were making between the cave and the pool.

There was enough light going into the cave, so we set the tools down, lit the lantern, and went in. "John, you are the builder, how should we proceed?"

John just stood there, looking over the entire chamber for a minute, and said, "This little cavern is shaped like a gourd. The entrance is not straight in from the center. As you come in, it has a gradual slope that rises about five feet. As you can see we have a slight depression to the right, which slopes up gradually for about twelve feet before curving sharply toward the ceiling over there on the far left. On the right of the depression it curves sharply up to the ceiling. Look at the rubble all over the floor; we could use it to fill this depression. We could level it out to create an oval-shaped flat floor about ten by fourteen feet. We could pave it with flat thin stones, like tile, and fill the cracks with sand. It could be very attractive.

"We could build a platform from where the slope curves sharply on the left to the edge of the floor. The platform will be about four feet high. We can build it with bamboo. Then we can add a light bamboo frame and hang a couple of sheets for a privacy screen. Whoever stays here can just walk up the slope to get onto the platform. We can make a mattress that can just lie on the platform. Later, we can build a table against the wall, some chairs, and a shelf. Also, if they want, we can create some doors or curtains to hide a storage area under the platform."

"John, that sounds wonderful. We should start by removing the rubble and filling the depression. Why don't you take the broom, John? Rob and I will take the shovels and get with the program."

An hour later, the rubble had been moved into the depression. We took the sledgehammer and tamped down all the jagged pieces so that nothing sharp would stick up. Then we went outside to let the dust settle while we looked for paving stones.

John surprised me when he said, "I told you I was a carpenter, but I was also a stonemason on the side. It was a hobby and a challenge. When a customer wanted stonework, I usually did it myself. These flat stones that are lying around will work nicely."

Rob and I carried the stones, and John set them in place. With the masonry chisels in his kit, he soon had a beautiful pattern designed out of the stone.

John said, "All we need now is some beach sand to fill the cracks and stabilize our stone tile. I will cut bamboo while you and Rob fill the buckets with sand."

Twenty minutes later, we were back with the sand. John grabbed an armload of bamboo poles and we went into the cave. We spread the sand on one side and tapped the stone lightly with bamboo poles until it felt solid. We kept sweeping the excess across the floor until we ran out about half way across. All the time we were working, we heard Jim hammering on the star drill.

We were about to go after more sand when we heard the drill break through. We heard Jim speak through the hole, "This rock is very hard but it is only about four inches thick at this spot. It could take several days, but we can make a big enough hole to go through."

I said, "That is great. We will meet you in the main cavern in a couple hours."

John started working on the platform while Rob and I went for more buckets of sand. When we returned, we finished the floor and went out to pick fruit for our lunch.

John had finished enough of the frame of the platform so the women could see what we were building. After lunch, Mary and Sarah were feeling better so we all went to the small cave. The women were amazed with the new stone floor. We elaborated on our plan to make a bamboo floor over the frame we had started, and a curtain for privacy.

Then I said, "Jim, Sarah, welcome to your new home."

chapter twenty-two

Vision for the Future

For a few minutes they were speechless. Then Sarah asked, "Why us?"

"Eve and I prayed about it and felt that the Lord was leading us to give it to you. Since you are the youngest couple here, you need the most privacy. We are used to the main cave and will stay there for now. If your home is ready on schedule, you should be able to spend your first night here tomorrow."

Rob and June agreed with our decision to build a bamboo house on the flat rock on the east side of the island. "We will give that to John and Mary."

John was about to get up but sat back down. "Why would you do this? You have been here longer and deserve the better accommodations."

"Well, John, we are used to this rough life. Soon you will be, too. God has blessed us so much. I have grown close to God since our arrival. He has led us this far. Why should I doubt what He tells me to do now? I trust that after we finish your home, you will help us with ours. All will be made right in God's time.

"God has given me a vision for this place. We will face many trials. But we will see the hand of God working on our behalf. Someday we will be able to access the mainland. God is assembling a team for the purpose of helping others get well. He has not revealed to me how many will be on that team. We are to make accommodations for many people. How many? I have no idea.

"I see that soon God will make a way for me to go back to the U.S. for a visit. Once there, He will provide additional training and a way for us to communicate with people around the world. He has revealed that He will be our protector and we need not fear men.

"You folks are a prime example of His provision. I am sure you can see that now. Somehow, when the real need arises, He will provide everything we need! For me to doubt that now would be a gross lack of faith.

"I am impressed with our ability to build without using up growing area for more than walking paths. We have to continue building in caves or in places where plants are not growing. I am convinced that there are many caves like the one we are giving to you, Jim and Sarah. There is no way that Rob and I could have found them safely. So what does God do? He brings us a mining engineer.

"We were led to build all these dwellings but none of us had any knowledge of construction or any tools. What does God do? He brings us a highly-skilled craftsman with the basic tools needed to create comfortable living quarters. What has been accomplished on your home Jim, tells me that, without taking away from our natural resources in the least, we could create twenty to thirty dwellings for guests to stay from a week to two months.

"I don't know who will come. But God, who makes no mistakes, brought us here for a purpose. You may, or may not, want to stay after we find a way to leave. You should pray about it.

"I would not have chosen this lifestyle or its isolation. But it has been our lot for nearly three months, and now I would not want to live any other way. I think that when I get a chance to go back, I will be uncomfortable with life in the fast lane. Eve and I never enjoyed life like we do now. Let us join hands now and pray together:

"Father God, we are weak humans and come to You as broken vessels, dependent on Your healing and guidance. You know what is best for us. We don't know yet what the future will hold, but we know You have a purpose that will benefit many others and us.

"Father, as we leave this meeting, we pray that You challenge us as couples, that You give us a glimpse of what You want us to do, that You give us peace, and increase our faith. Give us strength to face the challenges ahead. Give us wisdom to do the right thing in every situation. Lord, help us trust You without wavering. You, are our provider and strength. Amen.

"We will see all of you in the morning."

chapter twenty-three

UNITED WE STAND

When morning came, Eve and I entered the main cavern. Sarah and Mary were up and feeling much better. John had something important to say. "Adam, after the meeting last night, we talked and prayed. We cannot help but see the power of God in your life and your gift of leadership. We have never enjoyed this kind of camaraderie in the workforce. We believe that God brought us here to participate in His plan. We would like to run some ideas by you, if that is all right."

"Praise God. Tell me your ideas."

"Jim and Sarah feel unworthy of the cave but gratefully accept it. Also, I have some reservations about building on the spot you suggested because we would have to remove too many trees to get a good view of the ocean.

"An alternative is for Jim to find a cave on the east side, above the tree line, so we would have an unobstructed view of the ocean. If he doesn't locate a suitable cave, what do you think of building a home up on the mountain, with a lookout tower so that we have a view of the entire ocean around us?"

"Well, John, your ideas are sound. If we leave that flat rock hidden, it may be more useful as a secret, emergency, outdoor meeting site. I am all for having Jim start looking for other caves. In fact, Jim, now that you are familiar with the tunnel entrance to your home, can you look for adjacent caves that are close to the tunnel?"

"Yes, I can do that."

"Sarah, do you like rock climbing and hiking as much as your husband does?"

"I sure do, Adam."

"Well, we don't want him on the mountain alone. Rob's accident proved the potential for great danger. We were walking along the side of the mountain and he just dropped out of sight. He hit his head on the way down. If we had not been with him, he could have died before we found him. If you want to be his partner, we can concentrate on helping John and other tasks."

"That sounds great to me, Adam."

"Great, when we break up to go about our day, you two can start in the tunnel. Just mark any promising spots. When you finish the inspection, go up on the mountain and decide where you want to look next.

"The rest of us men will work on finishing your home. You will need a mattress of some kind. Do you gals have any ideas?"

June had one. "We can take two blankets, sew the edges together, and stuff them with the same kind of leaves that we used to make our other mattresses. The difference is that the leaves will not get in the hair nor move all over the place!"

"Great, June. In fact, if you like the result, why not make four more?"

"Why four? Are you expecting company soon?" she wondered.

"As a matter of fact, I do. It feels like a storm is brewing. Eve, Mary, do you agree with our plans?"

"Wholeheartedly, Adam, we are excited about the way God is leading."

Jim and Sarah went to the tunnel to search for other caves. Rob, John and I set out to finish the new home for them. Eve, June, and Mary were already making mattresses before we left. We carried in more bamboo. John went to work on the platform. Rob went back out to get more bamboo, while I worked at enlarging the hole into the tunnel. When Rob returned, we traded jobs. By rotating tasks, we succeeded in drilling a two foot diameter hole by noon. John was almost finished with the platform.

We were curious to see what Jim had found, so we all wiggled through the hole into the tunnel. We saw Jim coming up from below. He said, "I bet you want to know if I found anything."

"Exactly."

"Well, I found a good prospect right here, across from our cave. There are two other good prospects and four or five, less promising, potential sites. Of course, there is no way to determine their size until we cut a hole and get a lantern through so we can see inside. Anyway, this one seems to be much thinner than the one you just came out of. There is another potential cave entrance about halfway down, before the first turn where there is a bump in the ceiling. The second one is close to the opening at the lower end. I have to do some measuring, but the one in the middle lies under the site John wanted for a lookout tower."

"If they are as thin as you say, could we safely hit them with the sledgehammer and see if they let us in?"

“Yes, we can safely try that.”

“Well, let’s go eat and see how the other wives are doing.”

They were surprised to see us all coming from the tunnel. I flirted, “Eve, my darling bride, how did you ladies make out with the mattress project?”

“We have three done. We just added some fresh flowers. Three more are ready to be stuffed. We will have to walk further to get the filling material, but we should finish two or three more today. It is amazing what you can accomplish with enough willing hands.”

“Amen to that, my dear. The platform will be ready for the mattress in a couple of hours. We will improve the other homes as the need arises.”

chapter twenty-four

Discovering Possibilities

That afternoon, Jim, Rob, and I provided John with enough bamboo to finish the platform, before exploring the tunnel. Sarah stayed with the ladies to help finish the mattresses. Jim had been correct. The material in the three new cave openings was very thin and brittle.

Only two hits were required to make a hole in the site near the main cavern. In five minutes, the opening was large enough to enter. We found a room about one and a half times as large as the one we were preparing for Jim and Sarah. We could see where it may be close to the surface but could see no hole.

We moved on to the next site, which was overhead but within reach. It was like a great glass bubble covering another tunnel. We helped each other up and stepped into a large narrow room.

It was a little harder to enter the third site, but we were soon inside a small room with a flat sandy floor. We were turning to leave when Jim called us, "Wait a minute. I want you to hit two spots." Upon hitting the first one, an opening the size of a porthole appeared with leaves behind it. "I assume these bushes are beside the flat rock."

"OK, the other one is right here," Jim pointed it out. I handed the sledgehammer to Rob; he hit it twice and broke through. We had an opening into another long room.

I observed, "We could be in here a while. Let's see if John is finished. We should share our findings and include him in further discoveries."

John was just finishing the last piece of the platform. We pitched in and helped clean up the scrap. As we were removing the last of the trash, we saw our wives coming with the mattress. We took it in and set it on the platform. All of us were able to enter the room.

I suggested that the ladies join us to see our discoveries. "It will require a little easy climbing." They did not mind, so we helped them through the hole into the tunnel.

"OK, Rob, you are closest, would you take your lantern into the cavern behind you? Now you ladies can just peak into the opening and see the whole room.

"OK, Jim, let's help John go up into the next one with a lantern. Ladies, you can see most of this one. Later, we will build a ladder to enter more easily. We may be able to find an outside entrance. All the rooms we have found are dry. We have one more to show you. Follow me down here."

We entered a little room and turned into a larger one. I said, "We think this is under the tunnel. It looks to me like we have a series of rooms with thin walls between them. From what we can see, do you agree Jim?"

" Yes, it looks to me like the entire north end of the mountain is honeycombed with these low rooms. If we don't do anything to cause it to collapse we should be able to house a lot of people in here. I would say there are more than a dozen rooms as large as the one at the entrance. However, there is no way to know how many have access to the outside.

"I think you were also right to advise us not to walk around on the mountain 'til we were sure where it was safe. With the number of rooms we have found, in all likelihood there are other thin spots where a person could fall through. Once we locate them, they could make safe entrances or windows to let in light. We must avoid finding them Rob's way. Tomorrow morning, I would like to return to the upper chamber where we entered through the ceiling to check for any light coming through from outside."

I said "It is still early, is anyone ready for some watermelon?" With a chorus of "Yes!" we went out to the flat rock and ate watermelon until we were stuffed. We noticed that another storm was brewing. We prayed thanking God for our many discoveries and the good food. Rather than taking the usual leisurely walk around the point, we went back up the tunnel so we could get everything settled for the night.

We could hear it was raining quite hard before we reached the main cavern. Jim and Sarah got some bedding and went to their new bedroom cave through the tunnel. Eve and I decided against going out to the plane and stayed in the cavern.

chapter twenty-five

Mechanic on Duty

Timothy Ford and his wife Ruth set sail two weeks earlier with ten fifty-five-gallon barrels of aviation gas, his mechanic's tools, and spare aircraft parts. They knew of several mission locations that needed help. During the last week of sailing, there was very little wind, so they used their engine most of the time. While Tim was sleeping below deck and Ruth was taking her turn manning the helm, she did not hear the pirate vessel come up behind them.

Suddenly, a loud explosion deafened Ruth, and woke Tim. When she regained her senses she noticed the engine had stopped. Now she could see the pirate vessel coming alongside. As the pirates were about to board the boat, Tim came up on deck. Suddenly the pirates dropped their guns and left as if they had seen a ghost.

The pirate captain, Paco Menendez, had been robbing ocean vessels for thirty years, and his crew was a bunch of cutthroats who cared little about anything beside easy money. When they came up behind the Fords' vessel, they dropped a fast-moving inflatable skiff in the water from which one of the crew attached a magnetic explosive charge just above the water line on the stern. Once they returned to their ship, they hit the remote detonator switch.

They knew they did not have much time. As their ship came alongside the Fords' boat and the pirate crew was about to board, they saw a wall of twenty large warriors all along the deck. One of them reached out and grabbed the nearest pirate's gun barrel, bent it, u-shaped, like it was a piece of hose, and threw it on the deck. After seeing this, the rest of the crew dropped their guns and they left as fast as they could.

All the Fords could see were the horrified looks on the pirates' faces as they scrambled away. Tim shouted, "We better check the damage! We are taking on water, and the drive shaft is bent. It won't turn!"

Ruth yelled back, "Tim, what do you want me to do?"

Tim replied, "Pray while I think!" He then murmured to himself, "If I put the transmission in neutral, I should be able to start the engine. I have two drums of fuel in the rear hold. If I transfer those to the forward tank using the barrel transfer pump, we may be able to raise the tail a little. We have plenty of hose; that is where we will start." Tim yelled back to Ruth, "I can see a storm coming. This water will get very rough soon. We need to hurry!"

Tim put the transmission in neutral and the engine started. He got the bilge pump running and turned to Ruth, and said "OK, Ruth, take this hose and head for the bow. I will go below and get the pump into the first drum." Tim ran to the bow and removed the access cover to the tank. He yelled, "Ruth, hang on to this hose or it will jump out of the hole when I turn on the pump." He ran back, connected the hose, and turned on the pump.

After almost half an hour, the fuel in both drums was emptied into the front tank, thereby raising the hole in the stern above the water slightly. After Tim returned to the bow, he pointed out, "Ruth, the stern is raised and we are not flooding. But when that storm reaches us, all that will change. I think we can take the two empty drums and lash them to the bulkhead here on the bow and fill them with gas. Then we can continue to move two at a time up here and into the cabin. I think we can then use the transfer pump to assist the bilge pump to keep us afloat if need be. We are dead in the water. All we will be able to do then is pray and hang on."

So, together they moved the empty drums to the bow, tied them in place, and began pumping the gas back into the drums. Two hours later, with the ten barrels of gas transferred forward, they were about to close the hold and move into the cabin, when Tim saw a square piece of plywood on which the drums had been sitting. It had a hole in each corner and this gave him an idea. He tied the plywood over the hole in the stern. He knew it wouldn't keep out all the water, but he thought it might just keep waves from flooding the boat faster than the two pumps can get rid of the water. With that done, they closed all the hatches and waited.

The storm hit with a vengeance, tossing the boat violently. The bilge pump was able to keep the water out, so he did not have to contaminate the fuel transfer pump with salt water. In the wee hours of the morning, the seas grew calm as Tim and Ruth fell into an exhausted sleep.

The next morning at the cavern, Jim ran in and yelled, "Everyone come quick and grab some rope." So we went down to the beach. It was the strangest sight. Sitting in the little harbor was a boat with the point of the bow just under the water line and the stern completely out of the water. We yelled to ask if anyone was on board. A bleary-eyed man climbed slowly out of the cabin. We asked if he could catch a rope. He nodded. I threw a rope to him and it fell short. I tied a rock to the end and tried again. This time the rope end flew over the boat and he grabbed it. We told the man to tie it to the stern, which he did.

We all pulled on the rope, guiding the boat toward a sharp drop in the beach. The boat's bottom finally came to a rest with the stern now over land. The man dropped a rope ladder while a woman emerged from below deck. As Rob and I were starting in their direction to help them down, I turned to Eve, "Hon, will you get them some oranges?" By the time we helped them climb down, Eve was back with the oranges. They were quickly peeled and given to the newcomers. I asked, "Do you have some heavy rope we can secure your boat with?" The man pointed where to find the rope. We then went aboard and secured the boat to some trees.

While they rested, we introduced ourselves and I inquired, "Who are you and what happened to your boat?"

The man said, "My name is Timothy Ford, and this is my wife, Ruth. My friends call me Tim. I am an aircraft and engine mechanic. We were on our way to help several missionaries in South America when pirates attacked us." Tim told us how the pirates had set an explosive charge on the back of the boat, how the barrel on one of their guns seemed to bend by itself, and how the pirates then ran away.

And then Tim provided us with a revelation. "We have 550 gallons of aviation gas, tools, and a lot of spare plane parts." With that, Tim noticed curious smiles among us and asked, "What is it?" I told him, "We have been praying for your arrival for quite some time. Would you come over here a minute?" We led them to the area where they could see the plane. We explained to them how we came to be here, with no fuel or electric power. I remarked, "Except for being out of fuel and the electrical problem, our plane is in perfect working order.

We just need to remove this log and lower the wheels to roll it out to the water. With the tanks full, we should be able to fly to the nearest airport or boat dock." Now reflecting, I said, "You know Tim, you and your wife are quite a Christmas present."

Rob and the others told them about their encounters with the pirates, how their health problems brought them to this area, and that God had saved their lives. Rob said, "Tim, I bet those pirates that attacked your boat were the same ones that left us for dead."

As Rob and Tim chatted, I thought about how God had been so good to all of us. He had healed us of all our diseases just as He promised. Now He was providing a way to let our loved ones know we were okay.

Tim informed us that we were too far out to reach anyone on his radio, but also delivered wonderful news. "I am sure I could figure out what your electrical problem is in less than an hour. I also have enough hose to reach your plane. We can fuel it right where it sits without having to remove that tree trunk. I can test everything before we move it out."

I exclaimed, "That is great! We don't want to leave, but we want to let our families know we are all right and set our affairs in order. I would also like to establish some form of communication to contact our loved ones in the future. Our son knows a lot about that, I am sure he can set us up with everything we need. We could leave in time for Christmas!"

I then asked, "Can you fix your boat?"

He replied, "Yes. It will take two or three weeks but I should be able to do it. I may

need some parts from the mainland. I don't know how much damage we have, but I have the equipment on the boat to do the work."

chapter twenty-six

Ready to Go

Tim proved to be an excellent mechanic. He found that a short in the wiring had burned out the generator and the battery. He replaced the generator and the battery, and fixed the short.

While Tim worked on the plane, John went up to the cavern and came back with an ax, several pieces of wood, and a thin blade. None of us had ever cut a tree trunk. So John showed us how, and we soon had it cut halfway through by the stump. By then, John had already assembled what he said was a bow saw. He had the others start removing limbs and chopping up toward the top. Then he asked me to join him on the opposite side of the log where it was partially cut. In about twenty minutes, John instructed Rod and Jim to step back. A few minutes later, the stump flopped down and the trunk was just hanging in mid air. Rod and Jim had chopped a good bit by then. We took the saw and came up from underneath and cut up into it about 4 inches. Then we started cutting from the top. About fifteen minutes later, the trunk was on the ground. I asked, “Now what?”

John suggested that we all get behind the log and roll it. We moved it out about fifteen feet, even though the sand was very soft. The only problem was that it was rolling right into the path where the plane needed to go. Then John took a broken piece of limb with a tapered end about six inches in diameter, and placed it in the center, and said lets roll it onto this. Once we rolled it on the limb, John had us stop. Then he had me hold down on the small end and he pushed the large end and it spun around like it did not weigh anything. That made it easy to roll out of the way.

"Well, brothers and sisters, it is getting late. This log looks like a good seat. Jim looks tired and we need to pray:

"Father God, we can see without a doubt, that You are preparing this island, and us, for a healing ministry for You. Please guide us as we work to make this something special for You, Lord. Amen.

"Rob, you have been with us the longest and the others have specific work to do. Would you take over leadership while we are gone?"

"Yes, Adam, thank you for your confidence."

"I would like to come back with some kind of communications equipment. If we have a radio, we will need the antenna as high as possible. Jim, I would like you to find a good outside entrance to the upper cave we found to the north. John, please go with Jim and start making plans for at least a deck. It could be like a tree house with one spot touching the mountain. What I would like to see is a trail going past Jim and Sarah's house, past the entrance to the upper cave, up to the lookout tower, and back down to the flat rock.

"We could set up more screens and beds in the main cavern. I visualize that room as our main meeting room and the place where new people begin their journey back to health.

"I expect to be gone for about three weeks. I will learn all I can about the system of health we have been using since it has given us back our lives. I will bring back as many books as we can carry. I want to give my son power-of-attorney so he can take care of business for us in the U.S. I don't want to advertise. God has been doing a good job bringing us who He wants here, I think we can trust Him to bring those we will help.

"Ladies, please don't think I am leaving you out. When I talk to your husbands, I am talking to you. I think of you as a unit. There will always be activities that you ladies can do together while the men do something else. However, as we have stated before, we don't want anyone on the mountain alone until Jim has marked safe paths you can follow.

"Tim, I will not be able to haul anything large in the plane. If you plan to make frequent trips between the U.S. and the South American missions, would you consider this your home away from home and help us with supplies? We seem to be located beyond the normal range of the pirates. I hope God keeps it that way. We feel God is creating a healing mission here and we will need your help, if you are willing. Also, would you stay until we return?"

"Adam," said Ruth, "we would be delighted to be part of your ministry and will wait for your return. Besides, we may not have a choice. We still have many health challenges. However, from what we have observed here, we are confident that we will learn how to eliminate those ailments. Tim will check the damage to our boat before you leave in the morning. We may need you to get us some parts."

"By the way, Tim," I said, "John is an excellent carpenter. He may be able to help you patch the hole in your boat. Keep in mind, though, that he will most likely have a healing crisis and be out of commission for a day or two.

"We will need at least one contact person for each of your families to let them know that you are safe. Also, we need a list of necessities to bring back. Keep in mind that we have very limited space. The good news is that we will be able to make regular trips for supplies. Let's pray together and get a good night sleep:

"Father, the ten of us come to You in the name of Jesus, praising You for Your mighty deliverance and protection. You have protected all of us from certain disasters. We are all in Your hands and feel Your power in our lives. Lord, we have all made dumb decisions in our lives. We can't afford to make more. We come to You asking that You guide our every step and thought. Help us, Lord, to be in the center of Your will everyday. Amen."

chapter twenty-seven

Homeward Bound

At daybreak, we met by the plane. "I have a couple of parting thoughts. First, and this may seem out of place, but soon after our return, we could start having guests come for a healing vacation. People should not have to run out and hide behind the bushes to use the bathroom. Our healthy worm population makes short work of any waste, but some outhouses strategically placed are in order. They can be made of bamboo and could be moved occasionally. We could plant flowering vines next to them, and as the vines surround each outhouse, they will blend into the background. On the other hand, rather than moving the outhouses, we could build several so we can rotate the use of them.

"Second, I will look into getting a six-passenger plane to replace our two-seater. If we are making scheduled runs to a specific location, God could have guests wanting to travel by plane. We could also use the extra cargo space. A larger plane flies faster and has a better range, perhaps enough for a round trip. I have to research what is available and what we can afford.

"Finally, John, have you thought of a way to make a shower and a place to wash clothes so we can protect the purity of the pool water?"

"Yes, the parts I need are on the list."

"OK, if we tie a rope by each wheel and some of you pull it, the rest of us can lift and push so we can roll the plane to the edge of the water."

I was right. Even though the sand was soft, with ten people pulling and pushing, the plane rolled out of the enclosure and down to the beach with ease.

"Adam," said Rob, "we know you will do your best for us. Here is a basket of fruit for your trip. You have the list we made. We all wish you a safe, productive, and refreshing trip. We trust that God will help you bring just what we need."

"Thank you, Rob. Let us pray together. Everyone held hands in a circle:

"Father God, our parting this place is harder than when we left to come here. We have formed a close relationship in the short time we worked for our mutual survival. We don't want to leave, but we know we must. What we have here needs to be shared with others. We trust that our circle of dear friends will not be broken for long.

"Lord, please keep our brothers and sisters safe, as they work to prepare guest accommodations and homes for each couple here. Help Eve and I make all the contacts You wish. Guide us to the right equipment and give us the wisdom to know what to say to everyone we talk to.

"Lord, we know that You have assembled a team of Christians here. We also know that You may bring the lost here to receive healing. Help us know what to say to each person who comes so that no one leaves this place an unbeliever. We pray in the name of Jesus. Amen."

We got into the plane. When everyone was out of the way, I started the engine and confirmed that everything was working. Tim was a certified aircraft inspector and had checked all the mechanical systems.

We rolled into the water and were soon in the air. Since we did not know our whereabouts, we pointed the nose northeast and climbed to nine thousand feet. When we leveled off, we tried the radio and were pleased to receive a signal from St. Thomas. We adjusted our course and were soon with the friends that we were supposed to meet three months earlier, Dale and Sue Thompson.

The tower had notified them of our arrival, and they were waiting. After many hugs and tears, we walked to their car and went to their home. I said, "Before we visit, I would like to let our children know we are all right. Dale, could we use your phone?" We called our son, Larry.

"Larry, it's Dad, we are OK. We just landed at St. Thomas."

"Oh Dad! We thought you were dead!"

"Well, son, there is too much to tell you on the phone. Would you please contact your sister and tell her we will be home for Christmas? Would you also tell our friends in Jamaica and the Garza family in Cancun that we are leaving tomorrow? Also, would you contact our doctors and arrange an appointment for a checkup? I know this is a lot to dump on you, but we will leave here in the morning, spend a night at each place, and be home for Christmas Eve."

"OK, Dad, we will be waiting. It sure is good to hear your voice. See you soon."

When I got off the phone, I let out a sigh of relief, "OK, now we can talk."

Dale said, "We thought you were dead. You look like you were never sick a day in your life. What happened while you were missing? Are you hungry?"

"No," we said, "we ate in the plane." Then we narrated the entire story.

Dale said, "God be praised. So you intend to return to your island? We have not been doing well. I think we should visit."

"We would be delighted. Our accommodations are very rustic, but we like it. Dale, before you retired, you were in charge of purchasing, shipping, and receiving where we worked. Do you suppose you could help us with similar responsibilities now? We would like you to be our connection to the world. We would fly in monthly or as needed."

"If you let us be among your first guests, we will be delighted to assist you in making your ministry a success."

"Praise the Lord. Eve and I need to get an early start and it has been a long day; we should get some sleep. Let's pray together:

"Heavenly Father, we thank You for reuniting us with our dear friends, Dale and Sue. We thank You for the way You are working things out in all of our lives, for our good. We thank You for a safe trip here. We trust You for a safe trip tomorrow. We see Your hand of protection in unmistakable ways.

"Father, we see You working in a supernatural way to bring together a team of individuals who want to serve You.

"We pray that Your power will be evident in all we do. In Jesus' name, we pray. Amen."

chapter twenty-eight

Saving the Lost

Jim and Sally Baker met us at the airport in Jamaica. They were very happy to see us. I told them about all our experiences and how God had worked in our lives.

Jim said, "The obvious physical changes are phenomenal. I would not believe it if you were not sitting right here in front of us. As much as I would like to deny what has been happening on your island, I simply cannot explain it away. I think that Sally will have to agree that you have been right all along, there has to be a loving God in control."

I said, "Jim, Sally, we have talked before about Jesus and becoming a Christian. We love you and have been praying for you for many years, but especially since we left here. Would you be willing to accept Christ today?"

"Adam, we have been convicted of our lost condition the last three months. The scripture you showed us has been working on us. Yes, what do we have to do?"

"Jim, God is here right now. All you have to do is admit to God that you are a sinner and cannot save yourself, and acknowledge that Jesus died to pay your sin debt. You have to believe in your heart that

Jesus died, and rose again from the grave, to concur death, and pay your sin debt. Ask Jesus to save you and accept the free gift of salvation." Jim and Sally prayed:

"God in Heaven, We have seen through the lives of Adam and Eve and Your word that we are sinners in need of a savior. We believe Your word that Jesus suffered and died, and rose again to pay our sin debt. Please forgive us, Father. In Jesus' name we ask for and accept Your precious gift of salvation. Help us to walk in Your ways and increase our faith. Amen."

"Amen," I replied. "Jim, Sally, you need to get involved in a fundamental, Bible-believing church. I don't know what God has planned for you. We would welcome a visit from you on our island. We can offer nothing like what you have here. However, since your health is not good, we would like to show you what we have learned in that regard.

"We promised our children that we would be home Christmas Eve, so we need to sleep and get an early start. We would like to pray with you before we go to bed:

"Father, God, we thank You more than we can express for saving our friends, Jim and Sally Baker. We have been praying for them for more than thirty years, Father. We thank You for not giving up on them. Father, use them in your service. Bless them, Father, beyond their wildest dreams, in the name of our savior, Jesus Christ. Amen."

chapter twenty-nine

NEXT STOP, CANCUN

The Garza family met us in Cancun with smiles and hugs, praising God. When we were all seated, we filled them in on what had happened to us. We explained that we were planning to return to the island in three weeks.

When we told them that the Bakers in Jamaica had accepted the Lord and needed our prayer, Pastor Garza told me he would contact a pastor friend in Jamaica and ask him to help them.

"Adam, do you have any specific prayer needs?"

"Yes, brother, we do. We feel we need a larger plane. We would like a six or eight-passenger plane that could carry much more cargo. And although good people are running things, we would like for a doctor who understands what we are teaching to come and join us. Perhaps the Lord has a retired doctor, who is not motivated by money, all prepared to join us. If so, we need His help to find that doctor.

"It would also be nice to have a botanist either join us or visit from time to time to help us plan. We think the island will support about fifty people without cutting down any of the food trees. We believe we can build enough housing within the mountain for at least forty, including staff.

"We have a few trees we can cut up for lumber. It would be nice if the Lord helped us find a small portable sawmill. John is a very good carpenter, but he is very limited as far as the building materials he has available to work with. Bamboo is strong, but for floors, it is not very smooth to walk on.

"We are praying that our son can set us up with an effective communications system. We have no idea what the Lord has in store for us, but we feel the need to be able to contact the outside world." It was getting late and we had to go to bed. So I asked brother Garza, would you pray for us?

"Gracious Father, You have so wonderfully blessed us with the return of our brother and sister Westbrook. They have just outlined their needs to us. I have no doubt that You have ordained this ministry, Father. You are the great provider. You have provided their needs and, from what we can see, You have restored their health. Grant them traveling mercy and give them wisdom as they speak to others about this unique ministry on that little island. We thank You for Your bountiful love for us and seek Your favor, in Jesus' name. Amen."

chapter thirty

Home at Last

We were too excited to be tired. We flew straight through and only stopped for fuel. It was a long day but we arrived feeling great. Beside our family there were many members of our church who turned out to meet us on the beach behind our house. It was late Saturday, so I requested that the pastor let us tell our story in church the following day.

Our son, Larry, said, "Mom and Dad, we aired out your house and put fresh sheets on your bed. You look amazing. I can't get over how much younger you look. If I did not know differently, I would say you were only thirty-five."

"We have you and Sue to thank for that. Those books you gave us to take along became our guide back to health. There are no animals on the island so we were not tempted to kill anything. We did not even bother to try to catch fish. We simply ate an abundance of raw fruit and vegetables. We live on a small island which we have estimated to be four miles around. We have been walking and working to survive. God has been so good. We plan to return to the island in two and a half weeks.

"Larry, we need to talk to you about communications equipment, and we need some kind of power supply that won't damage the environment.

"You will hear the bulk of our story tomorrow at church. For now, I just want to say that God has given us a unique ministry. We have no idea what it will develop into. We have been living in a cave on a mattress made of leaves. As good as it feels to see you, Eve will agree that this does not feel like home to us any longer.

"We will be returning to the island to stay. We did not know where we were until a few days ago. All we knew was that we were in the center of God's will. We have seen many miraculous things in the last months and we will talk about them tomorrow.

"Larry, we want to appoint you as our representative here in the U.S. so you can sell our home and manage our investments.

"Sue, we want to learn as much as we can about the health system and take the information back with us. Have you continued to study the diet and lifestyle?"

"Yes, I have. My health has improved. However, I can see the advantage of being on an island with no other choice. My husband and children have not been too supportive of my diet change."

Sue's husband, Tom, spoke up, "Now that we can see what this diet and lifestyle have done for you, Mom and Dad, our girls and I will be more supportive of Sue. We can't deny the changes in your health and attitude. You just look so alive."

"Well, son, we believe that we were digging our graves with our forks. Now our fire is only used for heat and light. Don't you work for some kind of alternate energy company?"

"Yes, we have been installing wind energy systems to produce electricity."

"Praise God. Would you check into the price and availability of a stand-alone system? Tom, if God gives us a system we can afford, would you and your family be interested in coming down and visiting us while you install it? I know you are an electrician and we need help with wiring the caves for lights and possibly a pump for water."

Tom turned to Sue with a questioning gaze, and she said, "Dad, we would be delighted."

"Well, kids, this is all exciting, but it has been a long day and we have to get up tomorrow to speak to the church." We prayed together before retiring to bed:

"Heavenly Father, we humbly come before You praising You for Your goodness. We are in awe of Your power and provision. We are excited about what You will do for us tomorrow, and each day of the rest of our lives.

"Father, life used to be boring for us, but You have changed all that. Now we thank You for squeezing in a dull moment here and there so we can take time to thank You for Your blessings to us. In the name of Jesus, we thank you, Father. Amen."

chapter thirty-one

Our Home Church

When the opening song service was finished, Eve and I were called to the pulpit. We skipped down the aisle. I said, "I imagine that is not the normal way a speaker comes up here. Most of you saw us before we left nearly three months ago, and knew we were both in very bad shape physically.

"Some of you know that I had heart disease and prostate cancer. Eve had breast cancer, arthritis, and diabetes. We were scheduled for surgery the first week of November. However, God intervened in a miraculous way.

"Our health was good enough to allow us to travel. So to boost our spirits, Pastor Crane suggested we take a two-week vacation. He had no idea what would transpire.

"We were headed for our last stop before coming home. Being instrument-rated, I thought nothing of it when we entered a wall of cloud. Upon entering that cloud, we lost all electrical power. We later found out that a short had destroyed our generator and battery. That cloud became so dense that we could not even see our magnetic compass. All we could do was fly as level as possible, and hope we could find a safe place to land.

"Several hours later, we knew we had to be running low on fuel. Just as we exited the cloud, we ran out of gas. We saw an island below us, so we landed in a protected cove.

"As far as we can tell, no one has lived on that island before us. Our daughter had given us some books on health before we left. We did not have the strength to go hunting or fishing. We had all the fruit we could eat, so we picked fruit and read the books. The books told us God designed our bodies for a diet of raw fruit and vegetables. That is in Genesis 1:29-30, and I will tell you what it says:

"Then God said, "I give you every seed-bearing plant on the face of the earth and every tree that has fruit with seed in it. They will be yours for food. And to all the beasts of the earth and all the birds of the air and all the creatures that move on the ground - everything that has the breath of life in it - I give every green plant for food" and it was so.

"God spells it out very clearly in Verse 29, that we humans are to eat fruit, vegetables, nuts, and seeds. Since we found no animals on the island, we decided it was worth a shot and lived on nothing but the raw fruits and vegetables we found in abundance.

"I think that it is important to note that, in Verse 30, God gave the animals the plants for food as well. In neither statement did He tell man to cook his food while the animals eat theirs raw. From the evidence we have read, it is clear that the raw living foods we were designed to eat are the best choice for our nutritional needs.

"We lived in a large cave and started to walk a lot. At first, we went out just to get more food. Then we gradually exercised more and faster, until we were able to walk about four miles without getting tired. That's what the book, Health by Design, said we should be able to do if we were in good health. We knew our health was improving so we kept it up. Now it is part of our normal routine and we miss it greatly when we don't get our exercise.

"Then God in His wisdom brought us a couple who needed His healing. They were in the vicinity of the island when pirates attacked, disabled their boat, and left them to die in a storm. What Satan meant for their harm, God used for good. He intervened, and now they are experiencing health and life at a whole new level.

"When we were just two couples there, we discovered other hidden caves in the little mountain we lived in. Then God brought us a carpenter and a mining engineer. Pirates had also attacked their boat, and they, too, drifted to our island. While exploring the mountain together, looking for other caves, we grew very close and decided that we wanted other people to experience what we had found on the island.

"We continued to pray for an airplane mechanic with gas for our plane. You may have guessed it by our presence here; with the next storm, God brought us an excellent mechanic, with a lot of gas and spare parts.

"We are getting a checkup tomorrow to see whether our doctors agree that we are completely well. We have no doubt that we will get a good report. We also plan on returning to our island to minister to those who God sends us. We will guide them to the radiant health we enjoy. Our desire is to live out the remainder of our lives on that island. We expect to leave here within ten days.

"We are praying for a larger plane that can carry six to eight passengers plus baggage and supplies. We trust that God has the plane we need, at a price we can afford.

"On the island, our physical needs are few. We live a life with very few of the things we take for granted here. We have decided that we would like to have a few creature comforts for our cave homes, but we want to keep the island as unspoiled as possible. We will not clear land to build homes, which would remove the fruit trees and vegetable plants, that we live off of. We don't want to be in a position where we need to import food.

"If you and your pastor want to hear more about how God has miraculously delivered our little band of believers and provided for our needs, we can speak again tonight. We need your prayers as we follow God in this new way of living and ministering to the needs of sick people. Are there any questions?"

"Do you have pressing needs that you are hoping to fill while you are here?"

"Yes, we need a way to communicate with the outside world. Our son, Larry, is a communications expert, and we are depending on him to put together a plan for us to implement. The communications equipment will need electrical power. Though we appreciate the lanterns God has furnished us, we would like a renewable energy source that is non-polluting for the communications equipment and lighting. Our son in-law, Tom, is an electrician. He works for a company that sells wind energy systems. I would like to get a small wind generator set up on top of our mountain. We have a nearly constant breeze off the ocean, so it should work well for us. We have no idea regarding the cost, but we trust God to supply all our needs."

"Have you found this island on any maps?"

"No, we looked at recent maps and it is not pictured. It is not large enough to support many people, and we hope that no government challenges our claim to it."

"Do you expect to need any other personnel to care for the needs of the people God brings to you?"

"That is a good question. We are trusting God to provide for our needs. There is always the danger of accidents that need care. Therefore, it would be advantageous to have a doctor experienced in trauma care, who is also well versed in God's system of health restoration. Furthermore, we expect many visitors to be addicted to medicines, and imagine that some would need their drugs removed slowly. When Eve was about to run out of her diabetes medication, we started tapering off her dose until she was off it completely. We had no choice in the matter. We are convinced that God has the doctor we need, if we need one, and that He is preparing him for this ministry.

"Pastor Crane, we have run well over the normal service time. If you want us to return tonight to continue telling you about God's work on our island, we can. At this time, though, I would like to turn the service back over to you."

"Thank you, Adam. I know I want to hear more." He turned to the congregation. "Let's vote. If you want to hear more about the way God is working on that island, raise your hand. If you would rather hear a sermon from me, please do the same." The vote was unanimous!

That evening, we told them how God had used our testimony to bring our old friends to Christ. I explained that we would not limit our ministry to Christians. Our hope was that God would not let lost men or women leave without seeing His power at work and accepting his son Jesus Christ as Savior.

Pastor Crane led in prayer before we left that night. Many prayed for God's hand to be upon our ministry and thanked Him for our deliverance.

We went home rejoicing after the service. Our children and grandchildren were waiting for us. We had a great time in fellowship with our family.

Tom and Larry took me aside and said, "Dad, you are going to be very busy this week. Larry and I have been discussing your project. We need to know about how much lighting you will need."

"We need enough to move around safely, and some brighter light for reading. Our lanterns exceed our needs most of the time. We think we will have about twenty small cave rooms beside the main cavern. The light that comes in the dome during the day is enough to function, but it is not enough to read or to perform fine work efficiently. We only need the equivalent of night-lights in the tunnel. I think we can figured on two, 60 watt lights in each small room. We could set up five or six beds beside our own in the main cavern. Each bed will have a screen around it so a reading, or work light would be good by each bed. However, we want to keep it open for meetings and teaching small groups. If we set up a podium, we would need a light over it. So, let's say we need ten 60-watt bulbs in the main chamber. We would only use most of the lights about six hours each day. We don't know how many rooms we will end up with so let's say we need about 6000 watts per hour."

"OK, Dad, that gives us a good baseline to make a reasonable estimate. With a stand-alone system, you can use batteries to run everything, so the generator would just charge the batteries. If we send the batteries fully charged with you, they should last until we can set up your generator, but you have to use them only for your communications equipment."

"So what do you have in mind for our communications equipment?"

"Satellite phones, a computer with a satellite Internet connection, and a radio so you can communicate with aircraft or boats. We can have the phones and computer ready by the time you leave. The rest of the electrical equipment, the tower for the generator, etc. would have to be shipped by boat later."

chapter thirty-two

CHECKUP

We had a glorious Christmas with our children and grandchildren. We talked, played games, read the Christmas story, and had a great meal. While the main course was being prepared, we shared some melons from the island as an appetizer. Our daughter and daughter-in-law left off the turkey and trimmings for us, and we had a large salad with baked potatoes instead.

On Tuesday, we had our appointments with the doctors. They could not find anything wrong with us. They said they would have the results of the blood work before we left, but did not expect to find anything. They already knew Eve's diabetes was gone. They did a stress test on me and could find nothing wrong. In fact, I was told my heart was stronger than that of an average twenty-year-old.

Our doctors were amazed at our recovery. We told them about the others who had come to our island and recovered. They asked us whether we would mind if they sent patients to us from time to time. They were also interested in any information that would explain our miraculous recovery. Naturally, we offered to contact the publishers of the health material that same day.

That afternoon, we checked into our finances. We also contacted some people about a larger seaplane. The cost was way out of our budget, even if we sold everything. We decided to pray.

The words were barely out of my mouth when the phone rang. The man on the other end said, “Brother Westbrook, I would like to come over and talk to you about your ministry.” Twenty minutes later, we were seated together in our living room when he stated, “Brother Westbrook, my name is Don Flyman, and I was at the service Sunday when you narrated your experience. I have terminal cancer and would like to go to the island. I own an eight-passenger seaplane that I have been flying commercially for ten years. I have a proposal for you. I am ready to retire and would like a little amphibious puddle jumper. If you allow me to go to the island to get my health back, I will trade planes with you, an even trade, no money involved. Also, I have designed a way for you to pull my plane onto the beach since it is not amphibious. Are you interested?”

“Don, you are an answer to my prayer. We need the ability to fly several people to and from the island. What did you have in mind for moving the plane out of the water?”

“We could modify a boat trailer, with a winch anchored securely on shore, so you can pull the plane out of the water past the high-water mark like it was a boat hooked to a truck.

“You said you would be flying in and out of St Thomas. You could just tie up to a floating boat dock. You would not want to be there during a storm though.

The plane is a twin engine with variable pitch props designed so they can be reversed for maneuvering in the water. That would allow you to back up over your trailer under power. The plane has fuel capacity to fly about 2,000 miles.”

"Don," I said, "we would be honored to have you on the island. We don't have the money for such a plane. We just priced one, and it was twice our entire net worth. God has to be in this. There can be no other explanation. When can we see the plane?"

"How about Friday? You can also meet my wife, Jean, then."

We said that Friday would be great. We thanked Don and prayed with him before he left.

chapter thirty-three

Busy, Busy, Busy

The rest of the week was hectic. We talked to many people. First, we contacted Hallelujah Acres®, the ministry that published one of the books we had on the island, and requested the application for Health Minister℠ training and certification. We also contacted a Hallelujah Acres Health Minister℠ in our area. He was excited about our project, gave us more books, and told us about one of his clients who needed a place like the island to recover. The woman was not getting the support she needed at home. We offered to take her back with us and asked, "What is her name?"

"Charlene Johnson."

"Is her husband's name Carl?"

"Yes."

"She was in the service Sunday. We are meeting her tonight. We are old friends. Eve was her Sunday school teacher when she was a small girl."

"Isn't it amazing how God works things out for us?"

"It sure is."

By Friday we were ready for a break. Don had given us directions to his brother's home on a small lake. He greeted us and introduced his wife. He then took us around the house and out to the plane.

"She will carry eight adults, two crew members, and about one thousand pounds of cargo. This little lake is too small to take off with a full load, but I can take you up right now if you want."

We got in and were soon flying around the lake. After landing, I exclaimed, "This is fantastic. Praise God. Don, we will have to return to the U.S. at least twice in the next few months. Setting our affairs in order will take longer than we expected. So we are heading back to the island sooner than we had planned. Would you be able to leave next Monday? Will Jean be coming?"

"Yes, I could not leave Jean behind. She has suffered so much. She has rheumatoid arthritis and severe migraines. She wants to come and get well, too.

"I am a certified flight instructor for this type plane, so I can have you ready to take the written test when we come back. We can load some cargo here. If we have too many passengers, we will have to pick them up somewhere else."

"Good. We brought a book for you to read, but don't make any drastic diet changes until you arrive on the island. We don't want you to have a cleansing crisis on the plane. We have four friends who want to come to the island for their health, two in Jamaica and two in St Thomas. We may have one more who will board the plane here. Based on that, how much cargo can we load here before departure?"

"I would say about eight hundred pounds. We can stop at a boat yard I know on the coast to order the special trailer. They work on fishing boats, and I have done charter work for them."

"Good, we should be able to get the boat parts we need there. The way God works things out is truly amazing. Maybe Tom and Larry can deliver all the equipment down there by the time the trailer is ready. Our friends can take everything to the island on their boat."

On Christmas Eve, we had contacted the families of our partners on the island. Over the days that followed we gave Larry, our son, power–of–attorney to handle our affairs in the U.S. We also purchased supplies and weighed them, leaving room for the boat parts. We loaded the plane and were ready to leave on Monday. That Sunday, there was a dedication service for our ministry. We did not expect that show of support. We called our friends abroad with our new satellite phones and advised them that we were picking them up. We agreed on confirming our arrival time once we left the boat yard. We were ready for the slow lifestyle of the island.

chapter thirty-four

Return

Monday morning, Mrs. Johnson joined us at the plane. She was bent with pain. The Lord drew us to her immediately.

We said goodbye to our loved ones. It was much easier than expected. Eve pointed out that the peace we were feeling was due to our stronger faith in God. We knew beyond any shadow of doubt that He would take care of us. The fact that God had given us satellite phones, so we could call home from anywhere, also helped. We were not worried about being stranded and totally helpless. I prayed that we would maintain the close dependence on God that we had developed over the last three months.

We were welcomed warmly at the boat yard. They had all the parts we needed. Don gave them some sketches of what he had in mind. They agreed to build the trailer and promised to obtain the specs from the aircraft manufacturer to guarantee protection for the plane. They said we could pick up the trailer in three weeks.

We spent the night in a hotel and were on our way early in the morning. Since the larger plane was much faster, we picked up all the passengers and arrived in one day. Before the final landing, we circled the island once to announce our arrival. Our friends rushed to greet us.

Of all the treats we brought them, they were particularly thrilled with the twelve quality air mattresses with a foot-operated pump, and of course, with the phones.

After introducing everyone, we decided to move most of the cargo the following day. We secured the plane for the night and only carried a few items to the main cavern. We accommodated the new people and gathered for prayer:

"Dear Father, Master of the Universe, Creator of All Things, we thank You for what You are doing here. Lord, help us serve You without losing our dependence on You. You have provided for us beyond our wildest dreams. We love You, Father.

"Father, we have brought seven souls who need Your healing. Guide us Father, as we teach them Your plan for health and healing. Father, help them make this lifestyle such a part of their being that they will not stray from it when they return to their homes. We pray in Jesus' name. Amen."

chapter thirty-five

Settling In

We slept a very contented sleep that night. In the morning, while our guests were still sleeping, the rest of us met by the pool. I asked Tim, "How are the repairs for your boat coming along?"

"Today I should install the parts you brought, but we have to wait for tomorrow's high tide to push the boat out to deeper water. Then I can transfer the cargo to bring it back to level. A few hours and it should be ready to go.

"Based on your coordinates for the island, we can make the trip to the missionaries we originally intended to help in two days. If we leave you an emergency supply of gas, we can still provide them with 330 gallons. In one day, I can do the annual inspection on their plane. We should be back here in about two weeks to help you until we go back to the U.S. for any supplies for the island."

I was delighted. "That sounds perfect. Our son and son-in-law will have some equipment ready for us in about three weeks at a boat yard in Mississippi. That same boat yard is building a special trailer to beach the new plane. We were hoping that you could pick up all of this equipment for us and bring it back."

"Sure, that is no problem. We want to be involved in this ministry long term. We would like to make this island our base of operations, our home. We would like to continue going to South America to help missionaries with their planes, but we can also make trips to the states as needed."

"Tim, we greatly appreciate your help. By the way, we brought one extra phone for you to use."

"Thanks, Adam, that is unexpected."

"How many passengers can your boat carry?"

"When our boat was used as a fishing boat, it had crew bunks for six men, plus the Captain's cabin. It is far from fancy but we could take six passengers."

"OK, this is great."

"Rob, how are we doing with our construction and exploration?"

"Jim found an outside opening to the upper north room. We turned the opening into an entrance and cleared a safe trail to it. We are setting up our home in that cave. He also found ten accessible rooms in the lower part of the mountain. So far, we created an outside entrance for only one of those rooms in the east side. We started making quarters for John and Mary in the upper west room by the main chamber. They will have a good view of the ocean.

"Adam, we think that we should remove that big flat stone in the big cavern to make a more efficient entrance to the tunnel. We should let God worry about our safety and use the tunnel for quick access to our homes. Also, John built two outhouses so far. He can build more as needed."

"Eve and I feel the same way about our protection. Perhaps we should tip that rock today. One more thing, it sounds like all of you have homes now. We could quickly make a sleeping area in each of your rooms using the new mattresses.

"Mrs. Johnson is the only guest who requires a lot of care. She is crippled up with arthritis. She will require assistance to enter the pool for a swim, and needs to rest in the morning sun while we remove that rock. At least two of you gals need to look after her, and encourage her to take frequent short walks to build her strength.

"Our other guests have health problems too, but are fit enough and willing to help with some projects. They are all retired. Our friends, Dale and Sue Thompson, will help the ministry from their home in St. Thomas: they will let us use their dock to tie up our plane; they will handle the mail in our new post office box; and they will greet future guests at the airport and take them to the dock, where we will drop homebound guests and pick up new ones, as well as supplies.

"We have some equipment that should be ready in three weeks. Our family is coming here to visit and help while our son and son in-law install a radio antenna and a wind generator. We will soon have electric lights and a radio to communicate with planes and boats. We are also getting computers with Internet access. Your friends and loved ones will be able to e-mail you. My son will set up a website for our ministry so people who are interested can get more information.

"We brought five satellite phones. They can be used like walkie-talkies and can be useful in an emergency. Tim, we can order you a computer with e-mail, if you want. It would enable you to receive orders for supplies as well as letters from friends and missionaries by e-mail.

"One other thing, God used us to lead Jim and Sally Baker to Jesus. They are new Christians."

Everyone praised the Lord for His work. About then, our guests came out. Dale said, "What is all the excitement we hear in your voices?"

I explained, "We were just praising God for His many blessings to us. Let's gather fruit for breakfast and meet back here."

Twenty minutes later, we were all seated on the rocks by the pool. It was a good moment for prayer:

"Father in Heaven, we have no doubt that You are here among us. Help us serve our guests and bless them with Your healing. Use us to guide them in Your ways. Strengthen their faith, Father. We know You love us and will protect us from harm. Help our guests to trust You at all times.

"God, we thank You for Your bounty, which we are about to consume. In the name of Jesus, our blessed Savior, we pray. Amen."

The next three weeks went by without incident. A lot of work was completed. We set up two guest chambers in the lower caverns. Tim and Ruth went to South America and back. They stayed three days on the island and left for the U.S. All of our guests were doing quite well.

chapter thirty-six

Our Kids Come to Visit

When it was time for us to meet Tim and Ruth at the boat yard in Mississippi, our guests were all well enough to go home, except Mrs. Johnson.

We stopped in St. Thomas to set up our post office box. We landed at the boatyard that evening. Our son, his wife, and their four boys were there to meet us. Tim and Ruth had already loaded everything in their boat and were ready to leave. We had a meal on board before Tim, Ruth, our son, and his family sailed.

We spent the night in a hotel and arrived at the lake behind our house about noon. Sue and Tom were waiting for us. They had lunch ready. Don Flyman and his wife ate with us and then took possession of our small plane. He offered to check times and places for me to take the written test, for the twin engine plane, after my Health Minister℠ training.

Sue told us that we had been accepted into the Hallelujah Acres® Health Minister℠ training in March, and that she and Tom would be attending with us. We loaded the plane early the next morning and left with Sue, Tom, and their little girls, Grace and Hope. We were on the island that evening.

We introduced everyone. Sue said, “It’s no wonder that you don’t want to leave this place, it is so beautiful! We will probably visit often.” It was getting dark, so we showed them where to sleep and went to bed.

In the morning, Tom, Jim, Rob, and I went to the top of the mountain to prepare for the mounting of the new tower for the wind generator. There will be a strobe light on the tower. Beside the obvious safety benefits, the strobe light will help boats and planes locate the island at night.

We climbed to the top of the mountain. Jim showed us where he figured we should locate the tower. He said this is the strongest spot I could find. It is between the dome of the main cavern there and the north cavern.

Tom told us, “We brought some bags of cement and anchors to fasten the anchor pads securely to the mountain. If we can get the pads done by the time Larry and his family arrive with the parts, we will be able to assemble the tower and set it up in no time.”

I advised the others that Larry was scheduled to arrive in three days.

Meanwhile, Tim was coming back to the island on his boat. We could not have guessed what was happening to him at that time. When he returned he told us this story, as follows:

The first three days of the trip went by smoothly. The fourth day, at 4:00 a.m., I was manning the helm when I noticed the lights of another vessel. As we drew closer, I saw a distress signal. I pulled close enough to ask if anyone was on board. I heard steps climbing the ladder to the deck. Suddenly, I recognized the pirate that came out of the hatch. He was one of the pirates who attacked us. Then another one came into view. They looked sick and afraid. One of them told me that they were sick and that their engine had died. I offered to help them and they wondered why. One of them told me, "We tried to sink your boat last month, but the warriors guarding your boat frightened us away. Please don't come any closer."

I explained that we were servants of Jesus Christ and that their assault on us had turned into a blessing. I offered to tow them to the island to help them get well, and to repair their engine.

He was intrigued about my desire to help in spite of his past actions against me. I told him that God loved him and wanted us to help him. Larry heard me talking and came up on deck. I asked him, "Larry, would you throw that line over to that boat?"

"Yes", said Larry. He threw the line, and the pirate tied it to the bow. We continued our trip to the island, towing the pirate boat.

Our wives came up on deck. Ruth wondered, "Isn't that the pirates boat? Why are we helping them?"

I told her, "I felt compelled by Jesus. Something that pirate told me makes me think that they are open to the Gospel. Besides, I'm curious about what he said."

"What did he say?"

"He said that they were afraid of the warriors guarding our boat. I think that angels were protecting us, and God allowed the pirates to see them. We saw that pirate's gun barrel bend just before they left. I just feel like God has prepared the hearts of these men, and it was the only way they would listen."

Ruth said, "I hope you are right. We should pray. By the way, how far are we from the island?"

"Towing the pirate boat could add an hour, so we should be able to see the island within two hours." Larry prayed:

"Father, we have been told how You protected this vessel a month ago when these same pirates attacked it. Lord, we believe You have been working in their lives as well as ours. We believe that You want us to love them and help them. If we are wrong, Lord, please protect us. If we are correct, please use us to win them for Your service.

"Lord, we are totally dependent on You for guidance in this situation. Please work in the hearts of our brothers and sisters on the island. Help them to love these pirates. Let their love and testimony win them for You, Lord.

"In Jesus' name, we lift up our praise and petition. Amen."

chapter thirty-seven

New Babes in Christ

We were on the mountain working on the site for the tower when we saw Tim's boat. I noticed they were pulling another boat. I said, "We better get the others and a couple of rafts out there to help."

Tim saw us coming and asked us to come aboard and help. We went on the pirate ship, and Tim called, "Anyone alive down there?" We heard someone say, "Si, we are very sick, but alive." The air smelled very foul. The others went below to help the pirates, and I stayed by the hatch to help them out of the cabin. One by one, we brought all six of them on deck.

I addressed them, "You all seem to have a high fever. Before we talk, I would like to take you ashore to a cool spot and give you some fresh water."

"Gracias," was all one man said.

We helped them into the rafts and shuttled everyone to shore. We took them to the pool and gave them water to drink.

"Señor," said the pirate who appeared to be the leader, "we don't understand. We recognize many of you. We sank or tried to sink your boats, and we stole from you, yet you help us. Why?"

I replied, "Before I answer you, would you tell us what happened to you?"

The pirate said, "We robbed your boat (he pointed at Rob) and went to port to have a party. When we ran out of money, we went back out to find another boat to rob. We found your boat (he pointed at John) and took all your money for the next party. We lived it up for nearly a month and then needed more money. That was when we went out and found your boat (he pointed at Tim). When we came alongside to board your boat, there were about twenty huge warriors standing along the deck. One of them reached over and bent the barrel of my rifle as if it were as soft as a rubber hose, and pointed it back at me. My men saw this. We got scared and left as fast as we could.

"We still needed money. So, two weeks later, we went back out. We were well out of sight of land when our engine died. Our small lifeboat only holds two people. We knew it would travel faster with just one man. So we sent a man to get help. He never returned, and eventually we ran out of food. Four days ago, we ran out of water. We were hoping to rob whoever came to rescue us, but now we are too sick for that."

"What is your name?" I asked.

"Paco Menendez. I am the captain of our ship."

"Well, Paco, I believe that what you saw on Tim's boat were angels. You see, we are Christians. We serve Jesus Christ. Our Father, God, has been at work here. Because we serve God, we forgive you for your transgressions. God protects us. He brought us to this island and healed our diseases. God loves you, Paco. He is not happy with your lifestyle, but He loves you. He is using your wrongdoing for our good. As you can see, though you meant to kill our friends here, God intervened and they are safe and strong.

"God wants you to change your ways, Paco, and He wants to save you. We would like to introduce you to Jesus Christ, God in the flesh.

"Your lifestyle has made your body very toxic, and now your forced fasting brought about a cleansing crisis. Would you like to learn about God's plan for your health also?"

"Si, my men want to learn, too."

"God does not want you to perish. Jesus Christ died for your sins. Paco, you just listed many of your sins. Do you know what sin is, Paco?"

"Si, robbing, cursing God, killing, womanizing, and that sort of thing."

"That is right. Paco, God hates sin but He loves sinners. In the Bible, in Romans 6:23, you can read: For the wages of sin is death, but the gift of God is eternal life, through Jesus Christ, our Lord. Paco, the only way to have peace with God is to accept the payment Jesus Christ made for your sin by dying on a cruel cross. You also need to believe that God raised him from the dead. In Romans 10, Verses 9 and 10, God says: If you will confess with your mouth the Lord Jesus, and believe in your heart that God raised him from the dead, you will be saved. For with the heart, man believes unto righteousness; and with the mouth, confession is made unto salvation. Paco, do you understand that if you ask Jesus to forgive you for your sins, He will save you?"

"Si, my men also understand."

"Are you ready to accept Jesus as your savior?"

"Si, we are ready."

"Pray after me and I will lead you:

"Father, God, we are sinners. We have done many bad things. We know we cannot save ourselves. We ask that You forgive us for our sins. We believe that Jesus died for our sin. Please save us and make us new creatures in Christ. Thank you, Father, for saving us. Amen."

We all said in unison, "Amen. Praise God." I addressed Paco again, "If you were honest in what you just did, you are now my brother in Christ. We are all your brothers and sisters in Christ Jesus. As our new brother, we would like to welcome you into the family of God.

"Men, when you go without food, your body starts getting rid of stored poisons. That is why you are so sick. We will bring you a little fruit to eat and care for you until you're well in a few days. In the meantime, I will teach you more about health and God.

"With your permission, Tim will go aboard your ship, see what is wrong with your engine, and fix it if he can."

We took all four of our rafts out to Tim's boat and began transferring the equipment parts and supplies he had on board. When the smaller of the rafts was loaded Tim sent Rob and me ashore with a pulley and chain, pulling a line that looped back to his windless. When we had the pulley secured the line was tied to the other rafts and Tim engaged the windless. Using the windless He was able to pull the raft to shore, and then back to the boat, much faster than we could have paddled it. Soon all the supplies and equipment were on shore.

We all carried the supplies to the main cavern. We placed all the equipment for the tower at the base of the trail. We left the parts for the trailer on the beach. When it got dark, we went back to the cavern.

Our wives set up beds for the pirates and fed them some fruit. We all circled around them and I prayed:

"Father, God, we have given You control of our lives, and You are doing wondrous things. We don't know Your plans, but we thank You for our new brothers. We thank You for giving us the opportunity to rescue them in their time of need. Father, use us to strengthen them. Father, please guide them into your service. Help them turn to a new way of living and earning an income.

"I want to thank You, Jesus, for bringing our family to us at this time. We have much to accomplish before they return to the U.S. In Jesus' name, we ask You to bless our time together. Keep us safe from harm as we do this dangerous work. Amen."

Paco said, "Brother Adam, my men and I want to thank you for your hospitality. We don't deserve your warm welcome. Though we feel bad physically, we feel a peace we have never known. Thank you for loving us in spite of all we have done. Is there anything we can do to show our gratitude?"

"You should all be on your feet and feeling better in a day or two. We just thank God for using us to show you His ways. We have some projects that can use some extra muscle. We will talk more tomorrow. We all need some sleep. Good night, brothers."

chapter 38

Reformed Pirates

In the morning, we brought breakfast to the former pirates. They were able to sit up and were feeling better. I cautioned them against too much food or activity. Then I taught them that our bodies were designed to be nourished by raw fruit and vegetables. I explained that their cooked food and alcohol diet had filled their bodies with toxic chemicals, that their bodies were eliminating those poisonous chemicals, and that was why they felt so bad. Paco informed me that he could read English, so I gave him a copy of God's Way to Ultimate Health by Rev. George Malkmus.

Mrs. Johnson approached me just before we went out to start our work for the day. She said, "Adam, I see the power of God working on this island. Seeing how you folks took care of those pirates, in spite of all they have done, really had an impact on me. My pain is nearly gone. I expect to be pain-free soon. When you make your next trip, I will be ready to return home. I don't really want to leave, but there are others who need my bed. God be praised for his many blessings."

I said, "Amen. Thank you for your kind words. It is God who deserves all the praise."

All of us men went down to the beach to assemble the boat trailer. We anchored the wench well above the high tide mark. We backed the trailer down into the water, with the winch cable attached. We pulled in the boat anchors that held the plane and backed the plane up on the trailer. There were two padded uprights that guided it perfectly into position. We secured the tail and started pulling it out of the water. We were very pleased with the result. When we had the plane where we wanted it to rest we used a long pry bar Tim had brought to screw four anchors into the ground, one in front and one behind, of each wing. We then cut ropes to secure the plane to the anchors. I said the only thing that might make this better, is if we had some planks to park it on, so it would not settle into the sand, during a storm.

With that done, we went into the trees and got some fruit on the way to the cavern. There, we joined the ladies and our guests for lunch. Our guests were sitting up with smiles on their faces when we arrived. They were obviously feeling much better.

After our meal, I addressed Paco, "Why don't you go with Tim to your boat so he can see what is wrong with your engine? Also, we want to erect a tower for a wind generator on top of the mountain. We would appreciate it if your men would help us move all the parts up there." He said they would be happy to contribute in any way they could.

Since we had no way to raise the tower after assembly, we assembled it in place. By handing the parts up one at a time we were able to assemble all the braces and have the tower complete and all the bolts tightened by evening. With many hands moving parts into place, we were also able to mount an electrical disconnect box to the tower, and wire the tower. By nightfall, we were all ready to go inside and rest.

We ran into Tim in the cavern. He told us that he had figured out the problem with the boat engine and would fix it the next day since he had all the required parts. We prayed and got a good night sleep.

We woke up at sunrise and headed to the top of the mountain. John and Tom had already made a gin pole and attached it to the top of the tower, assembled the generator blades, and set the brake. When Larry's oldest son David saw the pole attached to the top of the tower he wanted to know what it was. Tom explained that a Gin pole is a long piece of wood or pipe, in this case Bamboo, with a pulley at the top used to lift items above where they are to rest. It had to be strong enough to handle the weight but light enough to be fastened in place by two men.

The wind was calm. We tied the rope they had looped through a pulley at the top of the gin pole to the generator and started pulling. We had another line from the generator to the ground, to help guide it. As John and Tom climbed, we pulled together and soon the generator was sitting securely in its place on top of the tower.

Tom had designed the tower with a box for our battery power system and its components as part of the tower base. The box had a floor about six feet by six feet, and fit between the tower legs. It had an access hole from below in one corner. The box was ventilated but rain tight. We passed the first battery up with a light. Once all the heavy parts were inside the box, John went back to work on the platform he was building for a home and lookout tower. Larry and Tom assembled the electric controls and mounted a circuit breaker panel so we could work on various systems while the batteries were charging. Eventually, we released the break and turned on the strobe light.

The next day, we mounted the radio antenna on the generator tower, and installed the radio in the upper north cave. John had set up a table for the radio equipment. Then Tim went to his boat, and I to our plane, to test the radio. It worked correctly. Next, we wired the north room for lights. Tom and Larry started running the electric wire for the rest of the mountain and they also mounted and wired the satellite dish for internet access.

After two days, Tim had the engine on Paco's boat running like new. Paco and his crew were ready to go home. They were relieved to hear that we would not be pressing charges against them. We offered to help them start a church if they could not find one. They thanked us for everything. We prayed and they left.

chapter thirty–nine

Giving up Our Old Home

The next weeks went by very fast. Our grandchildren were all home-schooled, so they never missed a lesson. By the end of February, we had electric lights in ten cavern rooms, and entrances from the outside for most of them.

John started building a small house on the platform at the top of the mountain. Rob and June took over most of the room under the tower. We partitioned off a room for the radio and computer equipment, and also for John and Mary to use in case of bad weather.

Everyone insisted that Eve and I take the big room next to the main chamber. We could not refuse. John built us a deck at treetop level and a bed frame. Larry included a surprise: a baby monitor for us to hear any problems in the main chamber.

Larry had his own business and maintained constant contact with his employees, but he needed to get home. I pulled him aside, "Son, I know you have invested all your capital into your business and you have been renting your home. How would you and your family like to move into our old home?"

"Dad, we would love it. Are you sure you don't want to sell it?"

"I'm sure, son. Your family can live there rent-free, and I know you will care for it as if it were your own. We need a base of operations whenever we are in the U.S., so all we ask is that you keep a room available for us. One more thing, it would be nice if you took care of our car so we can use it during our visits."

"Consider it done. Dad, thank you for your kindness. May God continue blessing you and Mom."

"The Lord is supplying all our needs so wonderfully, we don't need to liquidate our fixed assets. We would rather you use and care for all our assets, including our home."

"We will take you and your family to the airport in St. Thomas in the morning. Tom's boss is giving him another two weeks. We will bring him and Sue with us when we go home for the Health Minister[SM] training."

The next day, we flew Larry and his family to St. Thomas. Dale Thompson met us at the dock in his minivan, and we drove everyone to the airport.

Later, at Dale's house, we met Alvin Anderson and his wife, Trudy, as well as another couple, Tony Franklin and his wife, Donna. Dale advised us, "Alvin has colon cancer and Trudy has had a series of general health problems. Tony was diagnosed with leukemia, and Donna suffers from severe allergies, acid reflux, and a stomach ulcer. They heard about what God is doing on the island and want to see if God will heal their ailments."

I said "I was happy to have them join us on the island and we planned on departing two hours later."

About a week after Paco and his crew left for his homeport, Tim and Ruth went to South America. One of the missionaries they were helping was Pastor Matthew Cox, his wife Rachael, and their daughter Lora. All three were troubled with constant bouts of malaria. It seemed that one or the other was always suffering with some degree of it all the time.

The Cox family was worried that they would have to leave the mission field for health reasons. Tim suggested that they visit the island for a few weeks to see if our lifestyle helped. They agreed that it was worth a try. They needed a vacation anyway, so Tim put them on their boat and headed for the island.

As Eve and I approached the island with our new guests, we caught sight of Tim's boat entering the harbor. We circled the island to give him time to get out of our way and to show our guests the island from the air. We landed and backed onto the trailer. Rob, Jim, and John had us out of the water in no time. Eve and I were helping our guests exit the plane when Tim approached with a full raft.

chapter fourty

The Ministry Begins

We all met in the main cavern. I greeted everyone, "I want to welcome all of you to our island. One important rule: we ask that you never go wandering around the mountain alone, please stick to the established paths. We are not sure we have found all the hidden holes. If you stay on the paths, you will be safe." I asked the group to pray for each other. Then I asked the men to introduce themselves and their families and tell us a little about what brought them to the island.

Alvin started, "I have colon cancer. The doctors wanted to remove my colon. I heard about this place and I wanted to see if God could help me. My wife, Trudy, has gone through so many tests that I no longer keep count. The doctors don't seem to be able to figure out what is wrong with her. The medicines only provide temporary relief. We feel there has to be a better solution for our problems."

Tony followed, "I have leukemia. They say I need a bone marrow transplant but they can't find a match. Donna has severe allergies, acid reflux, and a stomach ulcer. I think she got the ulcer worrying about me. We live in St. Thomas and know Dale and Sue Thompson. They told us about this island and your ministry. We want to see if we can be healed."

Matthew said, "I am Matthew Cox, this is my wife, Rachael, and our daughter, Lora. We are missionaries in the jungle along the Amazon. We all suffer with malaria. Tim and Ruth told us about this place and what God was doing here. We wanted to see if God would save our ministry for Him through this diet and lifestyle."

I thanked everyone for sharing their stories and explained, "For the first few nights, we have beds for you in this room. We have found that most people experience a healing crisis within the first week of arrival. We can't predict what your crisis will be, but you could experience symptoms of the flu, cold, diarrhea, or a fever. Since we have no indoor bathroom facilities, we feel that it will be best if you stay close to those of us who can assist you, if needed, during your transition into this lifestyle.

"For example, Matthew, my guess is that your family will have a bout of malaria and Donna might have an allergy attack. The difference here is that we will give you no drugs to fight your symptoms. We will make you as comfortable as possible, and give you plenty of water to drink and some juicy ripe fruit if you are hungry.

"We have no cooking utensils or processed food. Everyone should understand that you cannot bring any medications or processed snacks with you. If this is not acceptable, we need to know now. If you want to leave, I can take you back tomorrow. We are about three hours from the nearest hospital. With that said, do any of you want to go back?"

Tony answered, "Dale explained all of this to us and to Alvin and Trudy. We understand and are willing to accept the risk." Matthew felt the same, "Tim made that clear to us. We left our medicine locked in his boat."

"Great. Now I want to tell you a little about God's health plan. According to Genesis 1:29, our bodies were designed to be nourished by fruits, vegetables, nuts and seeds, in their raw "living' state. Cooking and other means of food processing destroy the one nutrient we need most: living enzymes. It only takes a small amount of heat to destroy all the enzymes in our food. Our bodies have a limited potential to produce their own enzymes. If we eat predominantly processed, cooked food, we seriously tax the ability of our body to manufacture enough of these enzymes. Especially as we get older, our ability to create enzymes is diminished. As a result our bodies are less able to cope with stress and life in general. Disease is the natural result.

"Every process of life requires enzymes to keep us alive. They are the nutritional delivery system and without them, our cells starve. If the food we eat is loaded with living enzymes, our bodies are better nourished and have less work to do. For example, all the nutrition in raw fruit is in a form that is ready to be absorbed by the body as is. There is no digestion needed to change the nutrients to a form the body can use, and because the food is raw all the enzymes are intact insuring delivery of all nutrients.

"You have all read food labels. All those chemicals are toxic to some degree, along with the fact that heating alters the molecular structure of some of the natural elements in food, making them harmful. For example, frying turns fat from something useful to something that can cause cancer.

"With the raw diet eaten here, as provided by God, very little energy is used for digestion. Because of this, your body will have more energy left for removing the toxins that have been causing your health problems, and when this happens you experience a healing crisis.

Even though you will feel worse during a healing crisis, it is a sign that your body is stronger. I know this goes against worldly wisdom, but it is true.

"When you live the world's lifestyle of cooked food and sugar desserts, which are loaded with toxic chemicals, your body is often not able to remove the toxins as fast as you take them in. Your body will store excess toxins in your fat and other out-of-the-way places, like joints.

"When you improve your diet and lifestyle, your available energy rises, and your body starts to dump all the stored toxins. When your body is in the act of eliminating these toxins you will not feel well. That is what a healing crisis is. Your body will use any means it feels necessary to rid itself of the excess toxins and dead cells.

"Your first week here will be the hardest. Much like a drug addict, you will experience withdrawal symptoms. You may have other minor crises, but soon you will have your last one. From what we have learned, you will continue to improve as long as you don't go back to your old lifestyle after you leave.

"It may seem that I am spending a lot of time on the subject of the healing crisis. The fact is that your first healing crisis can be scary. You could get discouraged and want to cheat or quit because of something that may seem harmful. Be assured that your God designed body knows how to safely remove the toxins and diseased tissue. Your body has to remove the old diseased cells before it can build new tissue.

"We will give you books, like Dr. Howell's Enzyme Nutrition to help you understand what is happening in your body, and equip you for life after you leave here. You can ask any of the others who have been here a while. Once you get past your first healing crisis everything else seems to fall into place and life just keeps getting better.

"By the way, Eve and I will be leaving in two weeks. We are going to get more training and to talk to others about the ministry God is developing here.

"Let us pray together:

"Father, You have brought us seven guests. They are our brothers and sisters in Jesus Christ, our Lord. In Jesus' name, we ask You to work in their lives. Help them, Father, to grasp Your truth regarding health, to make it part of their being. Lord, please take away all their fear, and give them the peace that surpasses all understanding, which only You can give. Guide us as we minister to these dear ones. In the matchless name of Jesus we pray. Amen."

chapter fourty-one

Expanding the Ministry

By the end of the second day, the Cox family had malaria symptoms. We cared for them the best we could, and Matthew commented that he could taste the drugs the doctors had given him for the malaria. I told him that was normal. They were sick longer than the others. By the time the Cox family was on their feet, all the others had experienced some kind of crisis.

By the end of that week, everyone was walking around and feeling much better. I cautioned them not to overdo it, but to try walking more each day. I wanted to see them be able to walk around the entire island in an hour without being winded.

Both Matthew and Rachael Cox went through another mild healing crisis a week later. This time it only lasted a day.

The following day, we were about to leave for Health Minister℠ training when Matthew pulled me aside and said, "Rachael, Lora, and I feel better than we have ever felt after a bout of malaria, and it's awesome. I am sure some of our people will want to join us in this new lifestyle. We need to get back to our people. I expect we will leave before you return. Tim said they could take us back. Can we come again and can we send those of our people who need this kind of help?"

"Matthew, if some of your people need to get away from an environment that keeps them in bondage to disease, we are here to help them get free. Just have them contact Tim about transportation. We would also like to see you get the training so that you can minister to your people. When do you take your next furlough back to the U.S.?"

"We plan to return to the U.S. at the end of August for six months."

"Would you like to take Health Minister training Matthew?"

"Yes, that could be a great opportunity for me."

"OK, I will find out when the next training session is and what books are available. We will contact you when we return."

"I don't know how we can repay you. You have done so much for us."

Our other guests decided to stay another two weeks. We packed the plane and went up to the cavern to meet with everyone before we went to bed. I addressed them, "We are starting a new page in our ministry here. Soon, people from all over the world will know about it. We will return better equipped to help our guests stick with the program after they return to their homes. Let's pray together:

"Father God, we don't know what to expect or how we will be received. Lord, we still think we need a medical doctor to join our team. Perhaps one is coming to the training and is looking for a new start in life.

"Father, when we retired, we never dreamed of being involved in a ministry like this one, or that we would be living on a tropical island with a few new friends, without all the frills we once took for granted.

"We know Your power first hand, Lord. We ask that You protect Your children on this island, guide and protect us as we travel, and help us be the witnesses You want us to be. I pray this in the matchless name of Jesus. Amen."

chapter fourty–two

HEALTH MINISTER℠ TRAINING

Our trip to the states was uneventful. We landed at the lake behind our house just before dark. Our family was there to greet us. Sue had made arrangements for us to fly our plane to a lake near Salem, North Carolina, and rent a car. We spent the early morning with our grandchildren, flew to Salem, checked into our hotel, and got ready for the meeting that evening.

The Health Ministers℠ filed across the stage. They gave their testimonies first. That was a wonderful experience. We were the last couple to get up that night. They had planned on thirty minutes for us to give our testimonies and tell about our ministry.

It was hard, but we told our story. We mentioned that we prayed for the Lord to guide us to a medical doctor with experience in this diet and lifestyle, and with the desire to join us on the island. Brother Malkmus ran up to the platform and thanked us. He requested that we come back to the stage to answer questions when he was finished for the evening.

About two hours later, Brother Malkmus called us back to the stage. He gave people the choice to leave at this time. Everyone stayed.

I told the attendants about the pirate attacks on Tim and Ruth, how God had miraculously brought them to our island, and about the testimonies of all our guests. I explained that we needed to make it a place unlike any other.

We were asked how primitive were the conditions on the island. I explained that we lived in caves and had no indoor plumbing, but that now we had power for lights, for computers, and for charging radio and satellite phone batteries. Eve pointed out that we had no cooking facilities.

I told them we did not plan to invite anyone who wanted to transition slowly into all raw food. Eve said, "The only food available is raw fruit, some vegetables and whatever is ripe at the time. We have bananas, coconut, kiwi, melons, oranges, and several fruits we can't name." She told them that if a botanist wanted to visit to help us identify these fruits, we would welcome them.

A little over an hour later, Brother Malkmus came to the platform and proceeded to close in prayer:

"Dear Heavenly Father, we see evidence of Your work on that island. I am sure that many people need this place of isolation, where only Your bounty is available for food.

"We thank You for letting us show this couple Your health plan through our book. We know that the rest of this training will be a great learning time for everyone here. Lord, we ask in the name of Jesus, that You let this work flourish for You. Amen."

The next two days went by like a whirlwind. On the last day, while we were in fellowship with other Health Ministers℠, a distinguished gentleman came up to us with his wife. "Adam, my name is Dr. Frank

Dawson. This is my wife Loren, a registered nurse. We retired because of our health problems. The Hallelujah Diet & Lifestyle[SM] saved our lives. We have been planning to develop a health ministry with the Hallelujah lifestyle. We really don't want to get involved in a major project. However, your situation intrigues us. We feel the Lord leading us in your direction. Can we visit the island so we can make a decision? Anytime is convenient for us."

I said, "Brother, we would be honored to have you visit. If you wish, you can join us when we return. It will cost you nothing to fly down. Whenever you are ready to come back to the U.S., I will take you to St. Thomas to catch a commercial flight. We will leave in the morning to take our son and daughter back to their home. We will stay with them Sunday night, and we're planning to leave on Monday. Where do you live?"

"We live on the Mississippi and have a dock out into the river."

"You are only about an hour from our old home. If you give me directions, we could be at your dock at about 9:00 a.m. Monday." Frank gave me directions, described some landmarks to look for, and we said good-bye.

chapter fourty-three

Back to Our Island Home

The landmarks Frank gave me were good and we arrived on time. When Frank and Loren got in the plane, we introduced the others, "This is Saul and Linda Mason. Saul has rheumatoid arthritis, but his pain is not why they decided to join us. Linda has just been told her cancer is back and there is nothing they can do. She has already had a hysterectomy and chemo."

We landed in St. Thomas that afternoon. Dale met us at the dock with two couples: Chuck and Kathy Morris from Jamaica and Peter and Michelle McCain from Texas. I greeted them, "Welcome aboard. We will have more time to talk during the flight. We don't have lights on the beach and I want to get the plane tied down before dark, so we will have to get to know you better later."

We landed about forty-five minutes before dark. Once the plane was secured, we took our guests to the main cavern. Everyone was excited to see us and meet our new guests. I introduced our fellow servants and guests. The old guests were eager to give their testimonies to the new ones. Then I asked the new men to introduce their wives and tell us why they were there.

"My name is Chuck Morris. This is my wife Kathy. We are very encouraged after hearing your testimonies. I have bone cancer. The doctors said that if they had caught it sooner, they could have helped me. They told me last week I had about six months to get my affairs in order. Kathy has diabetes and a weight problem."

"I am Peter McCain and this is my wife Michelle. We were told we have AIDS. Michelle has it the worst. Her doctor told her that she must have received bad blood when she had surgery several years ago. Anyway, she is very weak and has been suffering a lot lately. The medicine makes her feel worse. Recently, they told me that I also had it, but we don't have the money to buy more drugs."

"My name is Saul. I have rheumatoid arthritis. Linda has just been told her cancer is back and there is nothing they can do. She already had a hysterectomy. They told her that she only has a month or two to live."

"My name is Dr. Frank Dawson. I practiced general medicine for thirty years, mostly as a trauma surgeon. This is my wife, Loren. She is a registered nurse. We retired because of numerous general health problems, and adopted the Hallelujah Diet & Lifestyle℠. We overcame all our physical problems and attended Health Minister℠ training with Adam and Eve. Their testimonies and the story of this place touched us. We have come here to see if God wants us to join this ministry. It is obvious that there is a need here and that God is working."

It was getting late. We needed to get our new guests settled for the night. I told them, "We will meet with all our new guests in the morning for breakfast. Rob, would you show Frank and Loren to our room after I pray?" I led in prayer:

"Dear Father God, Master of the universe. We finite critters stand in awe of Your power and glory. You truly work in very mysterious ways, Your wonders to perform. We stand in awe as we see how You get involved in our lives and the lives of those we touch. We see Your power displayed in their healing. We have seen many times how You have taken tragedy and created something special. Thank You, Father.

"Father, I thank You for Frank and Loren. We ask that You make it clear to them if You want them to join us on a more permanent basis.

"Father, we have all these new guests who have great needs. Help them to put all their faith in You and the lifestyle You designed for us. Use Your bounty here on this island, Lord, to heal all their diseases.

"We thank you, Lord, for Your marvelous provision for us, and for Your love and peace that surpasses all understanding. Guide us as we teach these, Your children, Your way to health. In the name of our dear savior, Jesus Christ, we pray, Amen.

"Eve and I are going out to the beach. We may just stay there tonight."

I grabbed a couple of blankets and we walked out of the cavern. We slowly walked down the path to the beach, holding hands. I felt physically drained, but so happy and content that I could not describe the sense of peace I felt.

We slowly walked to the south point, beyond the trees. We spread a blanket on the sand and lay together staring up at the stars.

"God is so good," I said.

"Yes," said Eve.

chapter fourty-four

The Continuing Story

Frank and Loren stayed with us two weeks. They decided that the Lord was leading them to join us. They went back to the U.S. to set their affairs in order and returned a month later.

Everyone who came to us sick, went home healthy. Even Peter and Michelle McCain, who had AIDS, went home with no symptoms. They stayed with us the longest of our many guests.

We soon figured out the quality of the fruits and vegetables on the island helped people get well quicker. We started teaching our guests about BarleyMax®, carrot juice, and other supplements to use when they returned to their homes, just in case naturally ripened organic produce was not available.

So far, only one person went back home and became ill again. Her husband did not support her in the new lifestyle. However, he later got sick and had to quit work. When she returned to the island, he came with her. A month later, they went home rejoicing.

We counseled all our guests to get in touch with a Hallelujah Acres® Health Minister℠ close to them so they could get ongoing support for their own lifestyle change and support the local health minister in their work in spreading the health message.

We also encouraged all our guests to become Health Ministers℠ if there was not one close to them. We went online and found who they should contact in their area, and made the first call for them.

I carried a steady stream of guests to and from St. Thomas on my weekly trips to pick up the mail. There was always someone there, ready to learn how to overcome disease.

Several months after Dr. Dawson came to work with us, we had a blessed surprise. The youngest couples working with us, Tim and Ruth, and Jim and Sarah, were childless when they retired for health reasons. Both women conceived within two weeks of each other. They both had their babies on the island. Dr. Dawson and his wife said they were the easiest deliveries they had ever attended. Both babies were under what is considered normal birth weight, but obviously, very healthy and were walking early. Neither of them has experienced any of the normal childhood diseases.

Life on the island has become quite routine, though far from ordinary. We have a meeting every morning and evening with our guests. We built quarters in the main chamber for the Dawsons. All the new guests start in the main chamber until we are sure they can manage on their own. After their first healing crisis, if they are fit, they are then assigned to one of the nineteen rooms we found in the lower area.

So far, we have not turned any guests away. God has healed enough people to make room for newcomers. We have not advertised but depend on God to control who comes, when, and for how long.

We give God the glory for all He has done in our lives. We praise Him for all those who visited the island and left rejoicing. Many of them are now teaching others how to get well and stay well without drugs and surgery, and are living rich and productive lives, beyond anything they could have imagined.

We were finally able to find our island on a map. It was unnamed and unclaimed by any country. Since we were all American citizens, and it is closest to the U.S. Virgin Islands, we have started procedures for the United States to recognize it. We are also working to incorporate it as a non-profit health retreat. It will be called "Hope Island" because it is a place of hope for the hopeless.

EPILOGUE

Have you found yourself wishing this story were true, and that such an effective health system existed? I am here to tell you that this system is real.

Tens of thousands of people, many of them just like you, have proven that it is real and that it works. Just like the characters in the story, they have adopted God's plan for radiant health and have been released from the bondage of disease. You can too!

If you suffer from disease of any kind, all you have to do is stop causing it, and it will go away. I know this sounds too simple. However, disease is caused. It does not just happen. We dig our graves with our forks and spoons, one mouthful at a time. We shovel in toxic chemicals and dead food, devoid of the live enzymes our bodies need for proper nourishment. Then we wonder why we get sick.

We rush off to the medicine man and ask for a magic potion to make everything better. So, the doctor prescribes a poisonous drug to chase away the symptoms, and we feel better. But, are we really better? NO. Though our symptoms may be gone, our body is less able to cope with the next challenge it must face.

God has clearly spelled out in His word what we are to eat to maintain health. All of God's plans are simple. We humans complicate His simple plan to our own detriment. By returning to His simple plan, as outlined in Genesis 1:29, you, too, can have vibrant health.

As the author I have set up a reader support website for you. If you would like more information about this diet and lifestyle or to contact me please visit www.sixmonthstolive.com

The Publisher, Hallelujah Acres® is a worldwide biblically based health ministry whose mission is reaching the world with the message, You Don't Have to be Sick℠. For almost twenty years, they have helped people from all walks of life, who were caught in the clutches of disease, turn their lives around and regain their health. The ministry's focus is educational, with Health Minister℠ training and certification programs offered three times a year, so that people from all over the world can learn how to be healthy, and how to teach their communities to do the same. They now have over six thousand Health Ministers℠ in all fifty states and thirty-five countries.

For information about Hallelujah Acres® seminars, Back to the Garden℠ newsletter, free weekly Hallelujah Health Tip℠ email, or to contact a Health Minister℠ in your area who offers support group meetings to help you live the Hallelujah Diet & Lifestyle℠, go to the Hallelujah Acres® website at www.hacres.com or call 1-800-915-9355.